THE LAND BELOW

WILLIAM MEIKLE

SEVERED PRESS
HOBART TASMANIA

THE LAND BELOW

Copyright © 2020 William Meikle
Copyright © 2020 by Severed Press

WWW.SEVEREDPRESS.COM

ISBN: *978-1-922323-77-4*

- 1 -

Daniel Garland looked up the mountainside and not for the first time on this trip wondered how in the hell he'd managed to get talked into this fools' expedition.

It had all seemed so straightforward back in London a month previously. A guinea a day for his services and all his expenses provided for had been the offer. He'd got a new pair of fine leather hiking boots, a new pistol—a .41 caliber Thunderer he'd had his eyes on for months—a gun belt and holster holding thirty rounds and a fine new saber and scabbard, all procured at no cost to himself from Holland and Holland. That was when he'd known that Ed Ellington was serious. It was also before he'd met Thomas Ellington; if he'd done that earlier on the first day, he might not have made it as far as the gunsmiths' premises.

It had started well enough. Ed Ellington had sought him out in Garland's favorite watering hole in town, The George in the Strand. Daniel had been sitting at the end of the bar minding his own business when a full tankard of porter was placed in front of him. He looked to his left to see a young, slightly plump fresh-faced fellow of some twenty years smiling rather awkwardly.

"The barman tells me this is your drink of choice. I'll buy you another if you'll listen to my proposition?"

"Son," Daniel replied, "I'll listen to any old bollocks if there's a beer in it for me, so buy away."

And at first, he did think the lad's story was nonsense, full as it was of talk of Teutonic Knights, lost treasure, and a hidden cave in Austria where all manner of fortune and glory might be found.

"So you're planning an expedition to this cave?" Daniel said eventually. By this time, he was on his third pint of porter and feeling more agreeable to nonsense. "Where do I come in? I know nowt about caves, I'll tell you that before this goes any further."

The younger man smiled ruefully.

"It is not your caving experience I need; I have a modicum of that already. I am more worried about both the journey to the place, and, if we are successful, the way back."

"Ah, I start to see," Daniel replied. "You need a guard?"

"Exactly. Someone to watch our backs and protect our interests."

"Now that I can do just fine. What's in it for me?"

Once the terms were agreed, Daniel had shaken the lad's hand and they'd both headed to the gunsmith's shop. After that, it was a three-course meal in the Ridlington Club in Pall Mall washed down with fine wines and brandy and by the end of that Garland was feeling pretty pleased with his new employer and the start they had made to their working relationship.

Then Thomas Ellington walked in. He was a tall, muscular, blond lad who carried himself with a cocky self-assuredness and swagger that Daniel recognized immediately. It reminded him all too well of young officers with more balls than sense and an over-inflated opinion of themselves. His suspicions were proved right when the newcomer ignored Daniel completely and spoke directly to his brother.

"I told you, Ed. We don't need him. I don't need him."

"And I told you," Ed replied. "I'll feel safer with him along."

"I refuse," the newcomer said. "I will not travel with a mongrel reject from the Army."

Daniel didn't get out of his chair but when he spoke, the whole room fell quiet.

"I'd be careful with my words if I were you, lad," he said quietly. "A lesser man than I might take offence."

The lad turned as if seeing Daniel for the first time. The color was high in his cheeks and his dander was up. Daniel knew that if he stood, the boy would take a swing at him. He also knew he could have the lad laid out flat in a matter of seconds. But he'd shaken on the deal with the brother so he held his peace and continued to speak softly.

"Your brother and I have come to terms," he said.

"Well, you can forget that."

"No, I can't," Daniel replied calmly. "We have shaken on it like gentlemen and I have taken my first payment. I'm his man."

Daniel saw that the lad was still ready for a fight. He sat back in his armchair and puffed at his cheroot, not taking his gaze from the youth's face. Thomas Ellington blinked first, reddened further, and turned on his brother where he couldn't turn on Daniel.

"Take it back, Ed. Right now. We don't need him."

Daniel watched both the lads closely. Thomas was the bigger, fitter, more cocksure of the two. But Daniel could see just by looking at them that Ed, although soft in the body, was the stronger in the head.

"I will not," Ed said. "As Captain Garland has said, we have shaken on it and he has taken a payment. He comes, or we don't go at all."

The brothers had stared at each other for long seconds then Thomas turned on his heel and walked out without another word. Daniel hadn't seen him again until all the details were ironed out and provisions were purchased, and he took to the train for Calais with young Ed one Saturday morning in June.

Now here they were almost a month later in an inn on the outskirts of Salzburg below the mountain and Daniel and Thomas Ellington had barely spoken a word to each in the intervening weeks.

"Tomorrow," Ed said as they sat on a porch having a post-supper smoke. "We're nearly there."

The three of them sat in a row overlooking the mountain, Daniel on Ed's right, Thomas on the left. Daniel saw that Thomas was wearing his pistol belt, a pair of Colt Peacemakers in the holsters, one on each hip. They were showy guns to Daniel's mind, too heavy when it came to close-range fighting.

Let's hope the lad never has to find out.

"It's up there. I know it is," Ed said quietly. The same words had been on his lips ever since they'd come in sight of the mountain two days before. The trip from Calais had been so uneventful as to be boring but here below the mountain, Daniel found the younger man's excitement infectious. He felt the old thrill and tingle that always came with the promise of action. The brothers began another of their seemingly endless arguments over a trivial detail of tomorrow's climb so Daniel tuned them out, puffed on a cheroot, and mentally reviewed their inventory for perhaps the twentieth time in as many hours.

They would be going in light, each of them carrying a rucksack with water and provisions for two days. They'd each wear a hard hat with a carbide lamp headlight fueled by a small acetylene tank that fitted at the top of their bespoke rucksacks. Daniel had eyed the equipment warily back in London when Ed had demonstrated it; going down into a deep cavern and trusting to a flame for light did not seem like the best of ideas, but the lad had been adamant.

"Monsieur Trouve in Paris has assured me that they have been produced to the most exact standards and I myself have tested one of them in Yorkshire just these two weeks passed. They work, Captain Garland. They work perfectly."

Of course, that remained to be seen.

"Are we expecting to meet anything in there?" Daniel had asked.

"Bear, possibly, maybe a wolf? I really have no idea."

Given the vagueness of that reply, Daniel had also decided to go in armed; he'd have the Thunderer, his gun belt, and carry a small box of spare rounds in the rucksack, extra weight he was happy to endure. He'd also wear the saber, having grown attached to it on the trek here from Calais. Thomas Ellington had also decided to go in armed, hence the Peacemakers.

Attached below the rucksacks each of them would carry a bedding roll and Ed, not being encumbered by any weaponry, would carry rope, a small paraffin stove and some pots and pans.

Satisfied that they'd done all they could to prepare, Daniel went back to enjoying his smoke and the view before darkness finally sent him inside for a good night's sleep in a proper bed. He intended to make the most of it.

- 2 -

Ed Ellington woke in the morning as excited to get going as he had been on every day of the trip. This was it, the culmination of a year of planning and fifteen months of fervent hope since that day in the Bodlean when he'd discovered the two loose leaves of parchment tucked inside the pamphlet on the geology of the Lamprechtsofen.

While dressing, his mind went back to that first afternoon back in a damp English spring. Tommy had been skeptical at first.

"It's a forgery, obviously," he'd said. "You know these medieval scholars; always happy to slip a joke in unawares, something to confound future generations. You've seen it before."

But Ed had the bit between his teeth.

"I've checked the dates where I could," he said. "And read the legends. I'm sure there's something to it. And besides, even if there is nothing there but the cave, it's still an adventure. That in itself is enough for you to buy into it, is it not?"

As he knew it would, his appeal to his brother's vanity worked its magic. Tommy agreed to pour some of the family's not inconsiderable fortune into the endeavor. Ed set about organizing an expedition to the deepest cave in Europe in search of a great treasure purportedly buried there by Teutonic Knights almost a millennia before.

And now they were here.

After dressing and before heading down for breakfast, Ed took out the two thin sheaves of paper for perhaps the thousandth time and reverently laid them out on the bed. He traced a finger along the line delineated on the crude map, from river to cave and into the depths. He mouthed the ancient Latin that told of the knight, Lamprecht, and his travels from the Holy Land, his flight from the Pope, and his descent into the dark. The short tale did not specify the nature of the treasure the knight had carried, but Ed had faith; it was there, in the dark, just waiting to be found. His head full of thoughts of fortune, glory, and a place in the history books, he finally put the papers away in an inside pocket and went downstairs in search of food to feed the body in the same way that hope had filled his soul.

Tommy and Daniel Garland were already there, and, not for the first time, were at loggerheads over something that had brought the older Ellington brother close to rage.

"What is it now?" Ed said on joining them at the table.

"Ask him," Tommy said.

Ed turned to the soldier and raised an eyebrow. He got a grin in reply.

"Your brother wants me to be head cook and bottle-washer," Garland said. "I informed him where he could put that idea."

"I pay your wages," Tommy said, almost shouting.

"That you do," Garland said pleasantly. "But my contract is with your brother here and nothing was said of my acting as your personal slave. If you want your shirt washed, wash it yourself."

Ed laughed and turned to his brother.

"You never asked him to wash your shirt?"

"It's dirty," Tommy said.

"Then wash it. Captain Garland is right. He's not your slave."

"You're taking his side?"

"It's not a question of sides. It's a question of personal responsibility and teamwork. We're going to need both once we get into the cave. If we're not of one mind, we're liable to come a cropper in a dark place where the sun doesn't shine."

"That's where I told him to stick his shirt," Daniel Garland said, and laughed as Tommy turned on his heel and left without another word.

"You should not bait him," Ed said as he tucked into some bread and cheese.

"He's a hothead," Garland replied. "That makes him an easy target. I have been avoiding him for that precise reason and today's little altercation was his doing, not mine. That said, I do not relish spending any time with him in a deep dark hole and I will be all the happier when this job is done."

"I think we all will," Ed said, and concentrated on his breakfast, his bright shining hope of just minutes earlier having already been tarnished before the day had properly begun.

It did not get any better when they donned their packs and ventured onto the mountain slopes.

"I say we go this way," Tommy said when they came to a fork in the path. He was pointing left. Garland shook his head.

"Right is the easier trail and ends up in almost the same spot if you look," he said.

"I didn't come to take the easy road," Tommy replied, and set off left. Garland shrugged, went right, and Ed followed the old soldier.

They met Tommy ten minutes later at a spot where the two trails met again some distance up the mountain. Tommy was red in the face and breathing in deep whooping breaths, whereas Garland and Ed were hardly breathing heavily. Garland smiled; Ed saw it but luckily Tommy was too busy trying to catch his breath to start another argument.

Besides, Ed had no time to mediate between the others; they had arrived at their destination. The trails had converged at what, in a wetter summer, would be a small waterfall with a pond below it. Now it was a man-sized gaping hole leading into the mountain with barely a trickle of water running out of the dark.

"This is it?" Tommy said when he'd recovered enough to speak.

Ed nodded.

"Exactly where the map said it would be," he said, pointing at the cave entrance. "It goes in, upward for a bit then opens out into the caverns proper. We're lucky it's dry; it might have been impassable otherwise."

"It might still be impassable once we get in," Tommy said.

"And we'll never know if we stand here wondering," Ed answered. He stepped forward heading for the entrance and was stopped when something moved inside, a darker shape among the shadows.

"Stand back," Daniel Garland said and pushed Ed aside. Ed noted that the soldier's pistol had somehow been drawn and raised in the second between Ed seeing the shadow and reacting. The pistol pointed directly at the entrance.

Something growled in the darkness of the cave.

"Do not shoot me," someone shouted from inside. "I am but a simple shepherd."

"Show yourself," Garland replied, and lowered his pistol as a burly man came out the hole with a large shaggy dog at his heel.

"I am Stefan," the man said with a thick accent and hit his

chest with a huge fist. "And I am here looking for a lost bullock. I was inside and heard you speak but did not show myself for fear that you were the very bandits who took my animal. But you are English gentlemen, are you not? Here to climb the mountain?"

The big dog at his side growled deep in its throat, eyeing Garland warily.

Garland holstered his pistol and reached out a hand to the newcomer.

"Danny Garland," he said. "English but no gentleman. And we're here to have a look in your cave."

The shepherd's huge hand engulfed Garland's and shook but he had a look in his eyes that looked very like abject terror.

"We do not go inside," he said. "It is not safe."

Ed laughed.

"And yet you were just in there."

"Only as far as the light would allow," the shepherd replied. "I cannot afford to lose a prized bullock. I needed to know if it had strayed inside."

"And had it?" Garland asked.

"No," the shepherd said, and this time Ed was sure it was fear that he saw in the man's eyes. "But something has been there. Have a look for yourselves."

Ed went to step forward and the big dog growled again.

"Don't mind Elsa," the shepherd said. "She's protective, that's all. Sit, girl."

The dog sat on its haunches, but its gaze never strayed from Ed and Garland as they walked into the cave. Ed knew before they reached it that something had died in there; the stench was unmistakable. He covered his mouth and nose with a handkerchief and moved into the gloom.

The thing on the floor of the cave inside the entrance had once been a mountain goat. Now it was little more than a crushed head and a carcass that had been torn asunder by some great force. Garland took one look at it and backed away outside. Ed looked over the top of the remains and into the deeper blackness of the cave itself before joining him; there was no sound but his own breathing but he felt sure that there was something there, watching and waiting.

"A bear do you think?" Garland asked the shepherd.

"There have been no bears around here in a hundred years. My first guess was wolf but Elsa here would have sniffed one of them out before now. And I never saw a wolf that could tear a beast apart like that."

"Me neither," Garland replied. "If I were back in Africa, I might conjecture it to be a lion or leopard. But there are no big cats in these parts."

"None that I know of," the shepherd agreed. "But there is something. And these slopes have long had a dark reputation."

Tommy laughed at that.

"I knew the locals would have a story to try to frighten us off. We came here to search this cave. Is one dead goat going to stop us before we even start?"

"Maybe it should," Garland replied.

"I knew you were all mouth and no trousers," Tommy replied. Ed stepped between them. Tommy hadn't seen it, but Garland's hand had gone for his pistol. Ed stopped it by placing a hand on the captain's wrist and turned to his brother.

"Put a stopper in it, Tommy. Of course we're going in. We just have to be careful, that's all."

"You be careful, then. I'll see you inside."

Tommy went into the cave without another word.

- 3 -

All of Danny's long experience and every bit of his gut instinct told him to stay out on the slopes in the light, to trust this shepherd. He'd tried bearding a lion in its den once in Kenya and still had the scars to show for it. Whatever had torn the goat apart might not be a lion but it certainly seemed to be as fierce as one. A cave was no place to fight such a thing. Given time, he might even have been able to persuade young Ed of the need for prudence but the lad was already on his way after the brother. As Danny moved to go with him, the shepherd put a hand on his arm.

"Please. It is not safe."

Danny patted his pistol and showed the man his saber.

"I know how to use both of these," he said.

The shepherd's gaze never faltered.

"They will not be enough," he replied, and seemed to come to a decision. "But you are guests in my country. I cannot leave you here. I will accompany you part of the way. Elsa will come with me, and she is a ferocious hunter. Mayhap together we can prevail."

"I must say," Danny said as they headed for the cave mouth, "I never expected to hear English spoken up in these hills."

The big man laughed.

"Benefits of a rich uncle and a good education," he said. "He wanted me to go to Strasburg and the university. But when my father died, there was no one to tend the farm but me. I was happy to do it."

Then there was no time for conversation as they entered the cave itself, having to step over the bloody remains on the ground to get access to the deeper darkness.

It took Danny a minute or so to get the headlamp lit. The dog, Elsa, growled as the tiny flame sparked, took and brightened, and only quietened when Stefan spoke softly to her in German.

By the time Danny was ready to move into the dark proper, he looked ahead to see the brothers' two lights bobbing some way ahead and upward, in a narrow tunnel with just enough headroom to allow passage.

They climbed in silence for several minutes with Elsa trotting just ahead of them, seemingly unconcerned at being in the tight darkness. Danny envied her sang-froid; as for himself, he was already casting longing glances backward to the receding dim light of the cave mouth. Even that small comfort was lost when the climb took a curve and the entrance was lost from sight. He had almost made up his mind to beat a strategic retreat backward when he saw that the bobbing lights up ahead had become still and fixed in one spot. A further short clamber brought Danny, Stefan, and Elsa out to join the brothers at an opening into a much larger cavern beyond. Their headlamps only lit a fraction of the space but it was obvious from the echoes running around them that it was a cathedral-like hollow in the mountain.

"We used to come this far as boys," Stefan said, his voice booming around them. "We'd bring bread and cheese and wine…and girls. We'd tell stories and scare each other a bit here in the dark. I haven't been here for more than twenty years."

"It looks like no one has," young Ed said, his whisper echoing back at them like the hiss of a snake. He looked down at a map in his hands.

"There is no way out save the one we came in," Stefan said. "Trust me, we looked."

Ed traced a finger along a line on the map and pointed to his right.

"Up, and over there," he said.

Stefan laughed.

"There's nothing there but a long drop into nothing," he said, his laugh echoing and booming around. "Your map misleads you."

Danny saw that the youngster wasn't going to be deterred.

"If your wee bit of paper says we go up and right, we go up and right. We've been following it too long to give it up at the last minute."

Tommy spoke first.

"That's the first sensible thing you've said since Calais."

And before Danny could reply, the elder brother was off again, clambering up a fall of loose rock on the right, moving fast and sure-footed with the misplaced confidence of youth. Ed went next and Danny and Stefan brought up the rear with Elsa now seemingly glued to the shepherd's heel.

"I am telling you," Stefan said. "It is, how do you say, a wild duck chase."

Danny laughed.

"In that case, our goose is cooked."

Stefan seemed puzzled at that but he obviously found Danny's laugh infectious and both of them were grinning when they joined the brothers at the top of the incline. They stood on the lip of a sheer drop. Danny kicked a pebble that rattled and echoed as it fell away into darkness. It was several seconds before the sound of its descent faded. If there was a bottom, the pebble still hadn't reached it.

"See," Stefan said. "There is nothing but death that way. We go now?"

It was Ed's turn to grin.

"If it's death, at least we came prepared," he said and

uncoiled the length of rope that hung below his rucksack. At the same time, Tommy reached into his own pack and came out with a small hammer and a bag of pitons.

"Just like Glencoe, little brother," Tommy said.

"Easier than that," Ed replied. "It's not snowing here. I'll go first."

Danny watched with rising horror as the younger brother smacked a piton into the rock, the clang ringing like a bell in the chamber. Once that was done, Tommy tied on the rope and Ed, without a qualm, lowered himself over the edge and let the rope take his weight. It made Danny go weak at the knees just watching. Seconds later, Ed spoke from somewhere below their feet.

"It's easy enough going," he said. "There's plenty of handholds, we've got a hundred feet of rope, and I'll bash some pitons in every few feet. Shouldn't be a problem."

"As long as it's not more than a hundred feet," Danny muttered. He turned to Stefan.

"It looks like this is where we leave you," he said, offering the man his hand.

Before the shepherd could reply, the dog at his heel let out a low growl that quickly became a bark. She moved to the edge of the drop and bent her head, looking down into the depths before letting out a howl that brought the hackles rising at Danny's neck. Stefan had to hold her tight by the skin at her neck to stop her from launching herself into the dark, but she kept growling, her lips pulled back to show her teeth.

"Something's got her spooked," Danny said.

"I've only seen her like this when there is a wolf about," the shepherd said, suddenly grave. "Mayhap your young friend should get back up here."

Ed answered from somewhere below with a laugh.

"If there's a wolf down here he's a better climber than I am," he said. "Just keep her quiet, would you? There's a good chap."

Stefan looked down the cliff then back at Danny.

"I will not leave you here," he said.

"You cannot follow us though," Danny replied. "We cannot take your dog down there."

"Why not?" Tommy piped up, and not for the first time, Danny considered punching his lights out. But it turned out for once that the elder of the brothers was right; they could indeed take the dog down into the dark. After Ed called up from the pit that he'd reached a ledge of sorts that looked to be a navigable, Tommy manufactured a basic harness from two shirts tied together and to Danny's amazement the dog went, as calmly as if sleeping on a blanket, down to Ed's side some twenty feet below. Stefan went next, hand over hand down the rope as if he'd been doing it all his life. Danny looked down into the dark and went weak at the knees. He'd stood in high places plenty of times with no qualms, but the darkness beneath looked absolute, a hell from which he might never rise. Every fiber of him shouted to flee. Ironically, it was Tommy Ellington that got him moving, or rather that supercilious smirk of his. Giving the choice of punching it or going down the rope, Danny opted for the rope…this time.

They grouped together on the ledge, waiting for Tommy to make his descent. Elsa growled again deep in her throat, looking pointedly along what looked a too-narrow ledge into the darkness to their left. Danny turned his gaze that way and lit up the narrow strip of rock they'd have to traverse above the fall. His lamp picked up something white against the rock, and while Ed cut off the rope to take everything save the twenty feet they'd used with them, Danny went to investigate.

He knew before he took two steps what he was looking at; he'd seen enough death to recognise it well enough. The thing that lay on the shelf had once been a man but that had been a very long time ago. Now there was only age-weathered bone and the rotting strips of what had once been clothing. A closer look told Danny something else—this had been no natural death. The rib cage was torn asunder and splayed, in much the same manner as they'd seen in the goat in the cave mouth. No matter how many years— centuries even—apart the two killings might have been, it looked to Danny's professional eye that the same kind of beast was responsible for both. But he still had no idea what such a beast might be.

Elsa seemed to have an idea, and she showed her opinion of it by lifting her leg and washing a stream of hot piss over the bones before once more taking her place at Stefan's heel.

"Well, we're down," Tommy said to Ed. "Now what?"

"The map says left," Ed replied.

"For how far?" Danny asked.

"As far as it takes," was the only reply he got.

- 4 -

Ed led them out along the ledge. It was only wide enough for them to proceed single file but there was little danger of falling; it was solid rock along its whole length and they were able to walk freely. It took them upward at a slight incline, a rock wall to their left and the drop into the black to their right. Ed was aware that his head was getting warm, hot even, a side effect of the lamp, but his excitement at being on the scent of the long-anticipated treasure kept him moving forward.

They continued upward for twenty minutes before Ed became aware of a cool breeze on his face coming from up ahead. At the same time, Elsa growled again deep in her throat, as if the breeze had brought a smell with it that she would have a disagreement with.

"Best let me go first, lad," Danny Garland said at Ed's back. "It's time for me to earn my keep."

As they shuffled past each other, Ed noted that the breeze was freshening in his face and now he caught a hint of what had spooked the dog, a faint odor of bad meat in the air, the same smell that had hung over the dead goat back at the entrance but coming from ahead of them. Ed was more than happy when he got moving again with Danny ahead of him. The old soldier had his pistol aimed along the trail ahead.

Minutes later, they came up and out into a cavern even larger than the first, a high-vaulted dome rising away and up into the darkness high above. Pale stalactites hung like ribbons from the roof, the dancing shadows making them look like grasping fingers. Off to their right, water ran with a rush. Turning in that direction, Ed saw a thin waterfall that plunged from on high into a pool that seethed and roiled as the water was sucked away in a whirl down to some greater depth. On checking his map, his heart sank; the path seemed to track directly into and through the waterfall itself.

He made to move in that direction but Danny stopped him with an outstretched arm.

"Me first," the soldier said. "There's a stench over there I don't think we want to get too close to."

As they moved in single file towards the waterfall, they quickly found the source of the smell; some of the missing entrails and organs from the goat was Ed's guess, a small pile of tissue and gore on a flat rock at the edge of the swirling pool.

To Ed's disgust, Danny bent and took some of the mess in his free hand.

"Still warm, but not too much so," he said. "Whatever left this here, it was sometime earlier today. There's definitely something in here with us."

Danny moved off to make a survey of the cavern. He went right, Tommy went left, but Ed only had eyes for the waterfall. The only way to it was across the pool and that was a seething roil of white spume. There was no way to pass, no matter how emphatic the line on the map looked. He was still staring at it when Tommy returned a minute later.

"Nothing but rock over there," he said then must have seen the look on Ed's face.

"Don't tell me. We're supposed to go that way," he said and pointed at the waterfall.

Ed nodded, not able to bring himself to say it.

"We go home now?" Stefan said hopefully at their back. Ed turned just as the shepherd took a leather flask from a shoulder bag, took a swig, and passed it over. Ed smelled the brandy before it got to his lips, and a deep gulp of it went down warm and most pleasant in his belly. He resisted the urge to take another and instead passed the flask to Tommy.

He addressed the shepherd.

"Yes, it looks like this is the end of the journey for us," he said. "Unless you know anything different?"

Stefan shook his head, took the flask back from Tommy, and had another swig for himself before putting it away in the bag.

"This is further than anyone I know has ever been inside," he said. "I know as little as you about this place."

Tommy asked to see the map so Ed passed it over. Away to the left, they could see Danny's headlamp, the light moving backward and forward across the rock. From what Ed could see from that distance, there was little possibility of an exit in that direction.

"Tea in two minutes," he called out, his voice echoing disconsolately around him, reminding him all too much of how empty the place was.

The small acts of getting the paraffin stove going and water boiling did a little to ground him back in a more likeable reality but by the time Danny returned with news that there was nothing but dead ends to the left, Ed was feeling sorry for himself again.

"I have dragged you all this way for nothing. A pipedream."

Danny grinned.

"Speaking of pipes."

He passed round his tightly hand-rolled cigarillos and soon they were all blowing smoke at each other save for Elsa who sniffed the air, snorted disgustedly, and immediately went to sleep at Stefan's feet.

"So what now?" Danny said as they drank the hot, sweet tea. "Do we look for another way in?"

"There is none that I know of," Stefan replied. "And I have lived in these hills my whole life. There is not even a rumor of another entrance."

Ed was barely listening. He'd looked down at his backpack on the ground and seen the rope, then looked up at the waterfall and the swirling pool.

"I have an idea. But you're not going to like it."

He was right, they didn't like it. Danny especially was vocal in his disagreement.

"Go into that maelstrom tied to a rope? Are you daft, man? To what purpose?"

Ed pointed to the map then to the waterfall.

"We go that way or we go home," he said. "I'm not ready to go home."

As he said it, he realised he believed it. He'd trusted the map until now and it had brought them this far. To give up now would be to deny the reality of all that had brought him this far. He expected Tommy to back him up, but his older brother appeared to have lost some of his cocky confidence faced with the reality of the whirlpool.

"I never thought I'd say this, but I agree with Garland, Ed. There is too much risk."

"And yet I have to try, Tommy. You see that, don't you?"

As soon as Tommy moved to take up the rope, Ed knew he at

least had his brother on his side. And it was Tommy who got the other two on board with the idea.

"You don't know him like I do," Tommy said, addressing the others. "Once he's got an idea in his head, there's no stopping him; it's how we got into this mess in the first place." He turned back to Ed. "But we do it my way, tied together alpine style, all of us or none of us. Remember?"

Ed remembered the climbs only too well but this was different, at least in his mind.

"It's only a bit of water," he replied. "Not a thousand feet straight down."

"Nevertheless, we'll be tied up. I insist," Tommy replied.

Seeing that it was the only way he would be allowed the attempt, Ed concurred.

Five minutes later, the four of them stood at the edge of the pool, all tied together at the waist by the stretch of rope that went from Ed to Tommy to Stefan to Danny in that order.

"We'll be anchoring you," Tommy said. "Don't do anything daft."

"You know me," Ed replied, and stepped off the rock into the cold, churning water of the pool.

- 5 -

It all went well at first. Ed, his only concession to the danger having been to divest himself of his backpack and helmet, moved slowly and carefully into the pool.

Danny saw Tommy pull on the rope so that he had his brother on a tight leash but as yet Danny didn't have to take up any slack.

"I'm okay so far," Ed shouted, having to yell to be heard above the rushing water. "It's dashed cold but I think I can make it."

The younger brother was having to put some effort into staying on his feet in the swirling currents and Danny saw that Tommy strained to maintain a stiff rope. Between them, Stefan put in some effort, his back muscles bulging as he worked to keep Tommy from being pulled into the pool with his brother.

"Nearly there," Ed called out. Danny saw that the man circled as close to the rim of the pool as he could, the swirling whirlpool sucking away at his right as he tried to navigate around it to the waterfall.

"He's going to make it," Tommy shouted, and Danny thought he might actually be right, but two things happened almost simultaneously that brought disaster on the whole enterprise.

Elsa growled deep in her throat and then let out a howl that filled the chamber. Out in the pool, Ed turned at the sound and immediately lost his balance. His footing went away from under him, the current caught hold and he vanished down into the whirlpool before he had time to let out a yell.

The rope ripped through Tommy's grasp, he took a tighter grip on it and was himself tugged off balance and into the pool where he was pulled inexorably towards the sucking whirlpool. Stefan planted his feet firmly and called out.

"Take the strain. Take the weight or they are gone."

The rope tore at Danny's palms as he took hold. He was looking at the shepherd's broad back, wondering whether the man's jacket might rip at the bulging seam, so he didn't see the thing that came out of the darkness to his left and barreled into the two men. Before he could get his bearings, Danny, with Stefan ahead of him, was tugged, hard, into the water. He caught a glimpse of Tommy going head-first into the whirlpool, tried to get his footing, then was dragged, accelerating, towards the suck of the pool.

Something white with a head as big as that of a horse and with a mouthful of teeth in a wet, red mouth lunged at him, jaw snapping shut only inches from his nose, then he was sucked away out of its reach.

He had time for one breath, saw Stefan go down into the whirl with Elsa leaping from the bank to go with him then he too was in the clutches of the current.

He went down into the spiral with no hope of ever coming up again.

The next minute was a terror plunge through whirling darkness; his headlamp fizzled out as soon as he went under the water. He spun like a child's top, buffeted, and pummeled. His left hip hit rock, hard, and his descent halted, but only for a second before the rope at his waist yanked at him and he was tugged away and down faster and more furiously than before.

His chest howled in pain, the last of his air gone. Something wet and soft fell in front of his face. Reaching up, he felt what he thought was the dog, Elsa, then it too was lost in the swirling madness.

This is no way for an old soldier to die.

That was his final thought. He was ready to give himself to the water and the dark when there was suddenly light beneath him. He shot out of the water like a cork from a shaken champagne bottle…only to find that he was falling through open air.

Below him someone screamed, long and loud. He fell for perhaps two seconds then hit more water with a thundering splash.

He fought, fearing that he might go under again, but found that his feet touched solid ground below him. He stood, water up to his waist, taking in huge gulps of welcome air.

It was only once he was able to breathe that he realised someone was screaming near his left side. He turned, and at first couldn't understand what he saw. Young Ed was holding off something that looked like a foot-thick snake with the head of a pony, mouth full of sharp teeth that were trying to tear at the man's face while taloned feet on muscular limbs tore gouges at his chest.

Danny reached for his pistol, realised that it would be too wet to fire, and was drawing his sword as he closed the ground between himself and the beleaguered lad.

Stefan beat him to it. The shepherd didn't pause. He stepped forward and grabbed the snake thing from behind, pulling it by brute force away from Ed's face and body. Elsa barked ferociously but was unable to go to her master's aid, her energy being spent on keeping herself afloat. Danny arrived at the shepherd's side just as the man's grip was starting to slip. The beast turned in the big man's arms and made a lunge for his throat. Instead, it met Danny's sword, a well-aimed thrust that went right down its gullet and emerged from the back of its neck in a spray of blood. All of the fight went out of the thing and it fell away. Elsa took the opportunity to swim forward and take hold of it by the neck, worrying at it as if it were a barn-rat.

As always was the case after action, Danny's sense of reality filled in slowly. The first thing he noticed was the cold that gripped like ice around everything below his waist. Then he saw young Ed was in trouble, blood seeping into his shirt from a series of wounds on chest and belly. He looked past the lad and saw what looked like a shore some twenty yards away. The older brother, Tommy, stood a few yards further away, head bowed and ominously still.

"Stefan," Danny said, putting the tone of his years of command into his voice. "Get young Ed to shore. We need to get out of this water before it kills us."

Getting all of them plus Elsa to shore proved more difficult that he'd thought it would, due to several factors; for one, they were all still tied together, his hip hurt like blazes where he'd bashed it, Tommy proved to be either in shock or had taken a concussion and had to be almost forcibly carried out of the water, and Elsa insisted on dragging the dead thing along with her, retrieving the kill as if she'd made it herself.

But finally it was done and they flopped out onto a shore of tiny pebbles. Danny kept on his feet as he got the rope untied from around his waist.

"Stefan, I need you to see to the lads here, okay? We need to get those wounds seen to, and we need to get dry and keep warm, so we'll need to get a fire going. I'll see if there's anything to burn around here."

It was only then that he took the time to check their

surroundings and he almost lost his breath again as he took in the sight. He had thought they'd somehow come out from under the mountain back into the sun, but there was only solid rock high overhead, a vaulting roof over a cavern that stretched away out of sight in every direction. Diffuse light, glimmering like a full moon on water, came from the roof itself, from pale luminescent roots that dangled in loose fringes from the face of the rock, waving in a breeze that shifted the roots like wheat in an autumn wind. A waterfall fell out of the roof and tumbled in a white roil out on the pond; Danny realised that was how they'd arrived, falling out of the sky from darkness into this near oblivion. The landscape around the pond was grey; bare rock and pebbles in the main, but as he looked closer he saw dry vegetation interspersed among the rocks; ropy lengths of what he guessed must be dead roots fallen from the roof above. He cracked one open with his hands and nodded to himself; it would burn readily enough.

He made several trips to and from the shore carrying handfuls of the stuff. Stefan was working on binding Ed's wounds with strips from a shirt out of Tommy's pack; possibly the same one Danny had declined to wash what seemed like years ago. The younger brother was awake and at least had some color in his cheeks, but Tommy was still lost in his far-away stare and Danny knew he'd have to check the youth out sooner rather than later. But his first priority had to be the fire.

He was amazed to find that his smokes and matches had

survived dry in the pocket inside his tunic. Using scraps of the torn shirt as kindling, he was able to get a fire going within minutes. The dry root burned slowly and he calculated it would be an hour at least before he'd have to collect more.

He finally had some time to take stock.

Stefan finished patching up young Ed.

"He will live," the shepherd said. "Most of the wounds are shallow. He will lose his right nipple, and there will be scars."

"But I'll live," Ed added, looking up at Danny from where he sat by the fire. "How's Tommy?"

Danny looked across the fire. He'd sat the other brother down, having to manhandle him like a mannequin. The blank stare that persisted in the elder brother's gaze had Danny worried but he tried not to let it show.

"He's had a knock on the head. Only time will tell. We can't let him sleep though; I've seen men in his condition slip away entirely once sleep took them. Keep him upright and awake and he'll come round in his own good time."

He knew that wasn't entirely accurate and from the look Stefan gave him, he saw that the shepherd knew it too, but young Ed had his own worries to keep him busy; he didn't need to take on those of his brother. Not yet anyway.

"My pack?" Ed asked as Danny passed 'round a smoke for each of them.

"Left above," Danny answered. "Along with the stove and cooking pans."

"…and the map," Ed said forlornly.

"The map's no use to us now anyway, lad," Danny replied. "We're in uncharted territory. Here there be dragons."

He pointed to the water's edge where the thing he'd killed lay in the shallows, already drifting away from them back towards where the waterfall plunged into the water.

"I have never seen anything like it," Stefan said.

"I'm not sure anyone has," Danny replied before Ed spoke up.

"You're from the North, Danny," he said. "Surely you've heard stories of the wyrm?"

"Old women's tales and bunkum," Danny replied. "Tall tales designed to make small boys fearful of going into caves alone."

"Not so tall though. Look at that thing and tell me it's not a wyrm. Lifted straight out of the old stories."

Danny had to admit the lad had a point. But it was a moot one.

"Whatever it was, it's dead now. Our concern here is not with it, but with how to get out of here."

Ed looked like he wanted to argue but he obviously lacked the energy. Danny saw that the lad's wounds were paining him.

"Stefan, do you still have the brandy? I think the lad could do with some."

The shepherd fished around in his bag that had miraculously survived the fall, and came up with the flask. He didn't pass it around this time, merely handed it to the youth. Ed took to it lustily. Two minutes later, his head drooped to his chest and he was gone into sleep that Danny considered to be a blessing. It gave him time to check on what else had managed to make the journey with them.

He still had his pack and his weapons. He'd lost the headlamp somewhere on the descent but that didn't worry him unduly while they had the luminescent light from above. What worried him more was the lack of food; Ed had been carrying the bulk of their provisions, and that was still sitting by the edge of the pool, somewhere high above and far out of reach.

He laid out his pistol as close to the fire as he dared to dry it out, doing the same with Tommy's Colts; in other circumstances, he'd have expected an argument from the lad, but all that was there was the same blank stare.

"This is bad, no?" Stefan said.

"This is bad, yes," Danny replied. "But I've been in tighter spots. We got in. We'll get back out again."

Stefan nodded.

"Elsa will find our way; her nose will lead her home."

That gave Danny another idea.

"How's her nose for hunting?" He waved an arm around, indicating the extent of the cavern. "Think there's anything worth eating down here?"

"Her nose is better than mine," Stefan replied with a laugh. He turned to the dog whose ears pricked up as he spoke.

"Rabbit, Elsa. Fetch rabbit."

The dog bounded away, soon lost to sight among the tumble of rocks to their right.

"If there is anything, she will find it," Stefan replied. "In the meantime, I have this."

He fetched some strips of dried meat from his bag. Danny laughed.

"What else have you got in there? A map of the way out? A telegraph machine?"

Stephan laughed again in reply.

"A shepherd learns early to be prepared for having to sit out bad weather…or mishaps in caves for that matter."

Danny looked at the roof of stone above them. The light seemed to be even and constant; there would be no nightfall here, just endless daylight.

He wondered how long they might have to survive under this perpetual gloom before they found a way home.

- 6 -

Ed woke with the taste of brandy in his mouth and a headache the size of London. There was something else too, something it took full waking and sudden saliva in his mouth for him to recognize. Someone was cooking meat.

He sat up and immediately wished he hadn't for shooting pain coursed through the myriad wounds in his chest and belly. He thought he might be able to walk, but only just. Running…or climbing…was going to need some healing before it could be attempted.

"The boy is back in the land of the living," the shepherd said and Ed heard Danny Gillam's laugh from somewhere behind him.

"Well, that's something at least."

Stefan sat up close to the fire, turning a makeshift spit that held something that looked rabbit-like if you didn't look too closely at the extra legs and too-long neck. The shepherd saw Ed looking.

"Elsa has been a very good dog. It looks like we are not fated to starve down here at least."

The dog lay at the man's side, gaze fixed on the cooking carcass. Her tail thumped twice on the ground as her name was spoken, but her attention never wavered; it looked like she was as hungry as Ed now felt.

"Tommy?" Ed said, looking across the fire to where his brother sat, head down, features hidden in shadow.

"He's much the same, lad," Danny said, approaching from the direction of the lake. "But he's alive. Give it time."

Ed turned slightly to look Danny in the eyes and winced again as the movement brought fresh pain. He felt tugging at the wounds but Stefan had bound them up tight and there didn't seem to be any fresh bleeding. Danny put a hand on his shoulder.

"Keep still, lad. We're not going anywhere for a bit, not until we know what's what with your brother. We have fire, food, and water and my pistol's dried out enough to give anything that might come at us a fright. Hunker down, we'll have some of…whatever the hell that thing we're cooking is…and we'll see if we can come up with a plan."

"What are we going to be eating?" Ed said.

Danny laughed grimly at that.

"I'm not a naturalist, so I couldn't tell you. It looked like a rabbit as you can see. But it had six legs, and a neck like a goose; ain't ever seen, or heard, of anything quite like it."

"What with that, and the wyrm, I'm thinking that these caves have their own ecosystem," Ed said.

"I have no idea what that word means. If it means there's weird critters down here, then yes, I'd agree with you on that."

"There's been no more wyrm sightings."

"Nope. And I've been thinking. If yon thing we killed managed to get out of this cave and up top, then we can do it too, somehow."

"Unless it didn't come from here at all?"

"Where else could it have come from?"

Ed didn't have an answer, and when Danny passed 'round a cigarette for each of them, they sat and smoked in silence, the only sound the spit and hiss of fat in the fire as the rabbit-thing cooked.

It tasted enough like a rabbit for Ed to be able to fool himself in the eating of it.

Stefan tried to get Tommy to take some meat, but the older brother was still lost somewhere behind his far off stare. He breathed, he blinked, but there was no recognition there that the world existed for him.

"Come back to me, Tommy," Ed whispered. "I can't do this without you."

He looked up to Danny Garland, more to look away from Tommy's dead stare than anything else.

"How long was I out?"

"Who knows? There's no passage of the sun to tell us. Several hours at least. Time for my pistol and shells to dry out. I dried your brother's guns too. Do you want them?"

Ed shook his head.

"Tommy will need them when he comes to himself again."

He caught the look that passed between Danny and Stefan; they didn't think Tommy was going to recover.

"What do we do if he stays this way?" he asked.

Danny took his time answering, and when he did, it was in a grave tone.

"I've seen men shake this kind of knock to the head off and be good as new, and I've also seen men just slip off into unconsciousness and never come back. I'd say it's a toss of the coin which one we have here. As for what we do? I said we need a plan, so let's have another smoke and talk through our options as we see them."

It turned out, however, that there wasn't a great deal to discuss. Danny laid out the extent of their surviving provisions—they talked about Ed's wounds and how long it might be before it was safe for them to travel and they all agreed that Elsa's nose was probably their best bet to find an escape. They didn't speak any more of Tommy's condition; all that needed to be said had already been gone over. As he tossed the butt of his smoke onto the fire, Ed looked again at his brother and said a silent prayer.

"Come back, Tommy. Please come back."

After eating and smoking, sleep called for Ed. He looked across to Danny.

"I should stay awake, help with the watch," he said. Danny patted him on the shoulder again.

"Stefan and I have got this; we've both got experience of long, boring watches to fall back on. Sleep, lad. Sleep and heal. We'll see about getting you on your feet when you wake."

He went down hard into the black again. If there were dreams, he didn't remember them, but when he woke it was with a start, as if emerging from a nightmare. Danny smiled at him.

"Back in the land of the living at last. And just in time."

Elsa had been busy again; another rabbit-like creature was roasting on the spit.

"She found something else too," Danny said softly. "Stefan and I pondered not showing it to you; you'll only get excited and I'm not sure you're up to it. But you deserve to see it."

"Now you've got me interested, you'd better show me," Ed replied, and sat up, too fast, bringing a flare of pain in his chest.

Danny took something from his jacket pocket and handed it over once Ed was upright. It was a gold ring. Heavy and regal looking and to Ed's admittedly unpracticed eye, it looked to be centuries old, at least.

"It's from the treasure hoard," he said, whispering almost to himself.

"I guess it must be," Danny replied.

Ed tried to stand. Fresh pain shot across his chest, forcing him into ignominious retreat back to a seated position.

"It's been where it lies all this time," Danny said. "Another day isn't going to matter. Elsa will lead us to it when you're capable."

Ed realised that he'd been so enraptured by the ring he'd forgotten to ask after his brother. He didn't have to speak; one look across the fire told him that Tommy was still lost inside himself somewhere.

"Has he spoken at all?"

Danny shook his head.

"The only sound has been Stefan here telling me his life story and I telling mine."

Danny rubbed at his eyes.

"We have been awake these many hours now," he said. "Are you capable of holding a watch for a time? I will only be napping and will wake in seconds if you raise an alarm; an old soldier's trick I've had plenty of occasions to test."

Ed nodded in reply.

"I can stay awake now as long as I stay off the brandy."

Danny laughed.

"There's no chance of you getting enough to get you drunk in any case; the shepherd and I polished most of it off; storytelling is thirsty work. Now, I must sleep."

The old soldier handed Ed one of his brother's Colts.

"Point this at anything that shows up and fire until it buggers off. I'll be awake after the first shot anyway."

Danny lay down and was lost in sleep within seconds. The shepherd stayed awake long enough to share the rabbit with Ed and Elsa, then he too lay down, the dog at his side, and both man and dog were snoring loudly minutes later.

Ed sat with the pistol in his lap, turning the ring round in his hand. There was an inscription inside the band but the writing was too small for him to make out without a magnifying glass and the only one he'd had with him was lost with his pack somewhere in the caverns high above. It left him wracked with frustration that he could not read it, which joined the frustration at not being able to be up and after the very thing that had so possessed him these long months. Then he looked at Tommy, and his heart sank.

"I'm sorry to have brought you to this, brother," he said softly. "Here I am thinking about treasure when it is you who should come first. I will not let my greed betray me again. I promise you that, on our mother's grave."

He slid the ring onto his right index finger; it fit snugly, as if made for it.

Time passed. Ed found the constant sameness of the light to be most disconcerting, and wished that he'd thought to take his pocket watch from his pack before what proved to be his foolhardy attempt to cross the whirlpool. That event, and the descent to where they now found themselves, was already taking on an almost dreamlike quality in his mind, as if it might be someone else's memory implanted into his. Then he looked across the waters, and saw the carcass of the wyrm still floating there. No, their problems were all too real.

I got us into this. I'll get us out. That's another promise, brother.

Despite his promise to Tommy, Ed's mind continued to betray him with thoughts of treasures that might be waiting somewhere in the rocks, maybe even within sight of where he sat. After a time, he could stand his own company no longer. He forced himself to his feet, having to stifle a cry of anguish at fresh pain in his chest. He finally stood, stretched to his full height, and breathed deeply, checking for broken ribs. There was indeed pain, but nothing too sharp, and the shepherd's bandages held.

"It seems I am to live," he muttered.

Now that he was upright, he was getting his first good look at the cavern. To his left was the waterfall and pond into which they'd fallen beyond which was an obdurate rock face. To his right, the view was more open. Although the roof dipped in places to almost touch the cavern floor, Ed was able to see that the cavern was at least several miles in both length and width, and possibly more, for there wasn't enough light to pierce the shadows in the distance. A stream ran from the pool away and across the cavern floor, which appeared to be mostly of the tumbled broken rock punctuated in places with what might be coarse vegetation or might just be more of the dried root material fallen from above. There was obviously life here; Elsa's hunting proved that much. Ed wondered what else might be waiting to show itself in the shadows.

He almost leapt out of his skin when he felt a hand press into his, and turned to see Tommy standing at his side. His first feeling was of relief.

"Tommy, you're awake!"

But as soon as his brother spoke, Ed knew his relief had been premature.

"It's time I got you home, Eddie," Tommy said. "Ma will be getting worried."

Tommy's voice was almost an octave higher than normal; just as it had been ten years previously, at a time when their mother had still been with them. She'd passed at almost the same time as Tommy's voice had broken. But now, for Tommy at least, neither of those things had happened. Worse than that, he appeared to be oblivious to their surroundings or circumstances. He tugged at Ed's hand.

"Come on, Eddie, it's getting dark."

"I know, Tommy," Ed said softly. "But we can't go just yet. We're having an adventure."

Tommy's eyes went wide when he saw the Colt in Ed's hand.

"Is that a gun? I'm telling Dad."

"Tommy," Ed said, trying to keep his concern out of his voice. "How's your head?"

"Hurts," Tommy replied. "That was a bit of a knock, wasn't it. We shouldn't play on that swing any more. It's not safe."

And with that, Ed knew where Tommy's mind had settled; he was lost in a country house in the north of England, on a hillside behind the property where they'd played as children on a rope swing where both of them had taken numerous tumbles over the years. Tommy was recovering, in his head at least, from one such fall.

"Is that a dog? Can I go play? Can I?"

Somehow, Tommy was simultaneously seeing Ed as his younger brother but also as an adult from whom he needed permission. Ed didn't quite know how to handle it; Tommy, on the other hand, seemed happy not to wait, let go of Ed's hand, and ran over to the sleeping dog, throwing himself on it with a giggle.

Ed had a sudden mental image of the dog tearing out Tommy's throat the same way it had done with the wyrm, but his worries proved baseless; the dog woke and immediately sensed the spirit of the moment. Seconds later, both she and Tommy were rolling on the ground, the dog licking at his face and Tommy giggling like a happy baby.

-7-

Danny woke with a start, instinctively reaching for his pistol and only stopping when he saw the wag of the big dog's tail and heard the happy giggling from Tommy, who appeared to be up and about, if not quite himself.

Young Ed stood off to one side, looking puzzled. Stefan had woken at the same time as Danny and was now trying to prise the dog and his new pal apart. Danny rose, stretched, and went to Ed's side as they watched the dog and the lad play together.

"He's awake, then," Danny said. "That is good news."

"Is it?" Ed said gloomily. "Is it really?"

"Put it this way," Danny replied. "Would you rather he were dead?"

The crestfallen look on the lad's face told Danny he'd been, not for the first time, too blunt in his wording.

"Sorry, lad," he said. "It's the old soldier in me I'm afraid. Look on the bright side. This is progress. He's had his brains rattled around inside his head. It's just going to take a while for them to settle down again."

"Really? You've seen this before?"

Danny had seen most injuries that could befall a human body over the years. He also knew that Tommy's chances of getting back to the man he had been before were middling to slim, but he couldn't bring himself to say that to the younger brother.

"Look, you're both on your feet. The best thing we can do for him is get out of here fast and find a doctor who knows what he's about."

Tommy, although within earshot, was too preoccupied with the dog to pay any attention. Danny saw a look of resolve pass across Ed's face, and knew that, for once, he'd said the right thing at the right time.

"What say we break camp and get on the move?" he said.

Stefan was already kicking dust and pebbles over their small fire, a shepherd's instinct for safety on the trail.

Tommy looked up at Ed and Danny.

"You're leaving?"

"And so are you, lad," Danny said, getting the youth to his feet. "We're taking Elsa for a walk. Do you want to come?"

Tommy looked at Ed and there was a childish, pleading, tone in his voice when he spoke.

"Can I, Eddie? Can I go for a walk with the dog?"

Ed had tears in his eyes when they all left their small camp five minutes later, but Danny thought it for the best not to comment on them.

Danny had taken charge of all the pistols. His backpack dragged heavy at him with the weight of the two Colts, their belt, holsters, and ammo along with them, but it was preferable to having them in the hands of a lad who appeared to have regressed to a mental age of somewhere around ten years old. This boy carried none of the braggado and swagger of the previous version but in truth, Danny wished for the older lad back, for there was something truly pitiful in what had become of him.

As for himself, Tommy was happy as a sandboy walking alongside the dog. Elsa seemed only too agreeable to put up with his ministrations and at least it was keeping the lad occupied. Ed walked beside his brother, lost in thought, although Danny was pleased to see that the tears had only been temporary.

They were following the stream that fed out of the pond, gradually walking down a slope further into the canyon. Danny's plan was to continue on this course and hope that the waters drained out somewhere outside in daylight, somewhere they could get out.

They had travelled only a hundred yards, picking their way across rock, when Elsa showed some signs of excitement.

"What is it, boy?" Tommy said.

"She's a girl," Stefan said with a laugh that echoed around

the cavern.

"Don't be silly," Tommy replied. "All dogs are boys. Everybody knows that."

And before any of them could stop them both youth and dog bounded away, heading off to the right away from the stream.

"Elsa, heel!" Stefan shouted, but the dog only came to a halt several seconds later. It stood on a small hillock of rock and barked furiously. They saw why as they got closer.

It wasn't a mound of rock, at least not a natural one. It was a cairn and it had served as a burial site in some distant past, but something had been at the remains. Bones lay strewn around the site alongside tattered remains of clothing and a sword long since rusted to little more than brittle dust.

"I think we've found where yon ring came from," Danny said, and Ed nodded.

"It was marked on the map," he said, almost to himself. "I remember now. It was just a name and I never knew what it meant. Jacques of Kassel. He must have died on the expedition."

Ed turned to Danny, the old zeal back in his eyes.

"Don't you see? We're still following the map. The knights came this way too."

"I see only too well, lad," Danny said and managed a grim smile. "I see that they also got out, for how else did the map get to England after that? There is a way out. We can all go home."

Danny gave Ed some time to rummage amid the ruined

tumble of the cairn but it was obvious there was no treasure buried here and nothing else to find beyond the ring itself.

"Did your map tell the way from here?" Stefan asked, twice before Ed replied.

"It followed the stream after this." He pointed down the slope towards the distant shadows. "That way."

"It's the way we're going anyway," Danny replied.

Even then, Ed looked to be reluctant to be on the move. It took Tommy and Elsa to get him away and walking; the dog went first, bounding down the slope with Tommy whooping like a banshee at her heels. Several of the rabbit-like things, flushed from the rocks, scattered to all points of the compass, one of them only eluding Elsa by the thinnest of hairs on its back legs.

"There is plenty of food, at least that's something," Stefan said.

Danny was looking further down the slope; another movement had caught his eye. His hand went to his pistol at first, then away again when he realised what he was seeing.

The rock ceiling came down closer to the cavern floor at the foot of the slope and there were beasts down there taking advantage of that fact to feed on the pale roots that dangled down. At first, Danny thought them to be some kind of giraffe, impossibly transplanted from the African plains to this lost cavern. Then he got a better look as one turned to gaze up the hill at the approaching men.

It had the torso and head of a horse and in bulk was the size of a large pony but there the equine resemblances ended. The neck, while not as long as that of a giraffe, was definitely elongated in the same manner as they'd already seen in the 'rabbits.' And again, there were too many legs, six in total, three to a side and bent outward at what might be knees to give it an almost crab-like, scuttling gait as the small herd of perhaps a score of the pale beasts retreated at the same pace as the men advanced towards them. Elsa barked excitedly and that was the cue for the herd to turn as one and flee, off and away into deeper gloom below.

Elsa would have followed had Stefan not brought her to heel with a sharp word that saw her creep back, tail between her legs. Tommy, meanwhile, showed no contrition.

"Horses, Eddie. Can I ride one?"

That finally got a laugh from his brother.

"Tell you what, Tommy, if you can get one of those things to let you on its back, I'll be the first to congratulate you."

Tommy looked confused at first, then immediately forgot his thread of thought as Elsa nuzzled her head into his palm for him to pet her.

They arrived at the point where the herd had been feeding a few minutes later. Before any of them could stop him, Tommy reached up, grabbed one of the dangling roots, pulled it out of the rock, bit a chunk from it, and chewed.

The look on his face as he spit it out almost made Danny laugh.

"What's the matter, lad? Is it bitter?"

"It tastes like cabbage. Tommy hates cabbage."

Danny took the root from the youth. In texture, it felt pulpy, like a soft turnip, and there was a faint vinegary smell coming from it. Danny took a tentative bite. It wasn't too unpleasant in the mouth and did indeed taste like cabbage.

"If we run out of rabbits, this should sustain us," he said.

Tommy put two fingers down his throat and feigned vomiting.

"Cabbage. Yuk. It smells like hot wee."

That did get a laugh from all of them, and in spite of their situation, their spirits were high as they continued down the slope, still following the track of the stream.

The roof lifted up and away from them again, exposing an even larger extent of the cavern below them. There was more ground cover vegetation here, wispy pale grass in the main punctuated with thickets of something that looked like gorse.

"Are we heading inward deeper into the mountain, or outward towards the village?" Ed asked.

Danny shrugged.

"You had the compass and it's up in your pack where you left it. There's no way to tell without the sun or stars to guide us. My

THE LAND BELOW

gut says we're going deeper into the mountain…but my gut's been known to be wrong."

Stefan spoke up.

"I've done more than my share of walking these lands under very heavy clouds," he said. "And my belly, ample as it is, tells me we are going the wrong way. But we are following the water, no? It will find a way. Water always does."

"Are we going home now, Eddie?" Tommy said. "I don't like this place anymore. It doesn't smell right."

"Like warm wee?" Danny said with a smile.

"No, like something died," Tommy said, and pointed ahead of them on the trail. They had been too busy talking to notice it, and it was partially obscured by a patch of the gorse, but as they stepped closer, they saw that one of the horse-things lay there dead.

"Keep Tommy back," Danny said to Ed. "He shouldn't see this."

Danny walked forward, his hand back on his pistol.

It was a fresh kill and the poor thing had been opened from throat to belly, its ribs torn wide open as something had ripped it apart in the same manner as they'd seen in the dead goat at the entrance to the cavern high above.

"Yon thing we left in the water was dead, right?" he said to Stefan who had stepped up to join him.

"You yourself put a sword through its brain and Elsa worried

56

at it long after that. It was as dead as anything I have ever seen."

Danny smiled grimly.

"Just checking. This looks like the work of the same beast, in which case there are more of those wormy buggers around here somewhere. We need to be more careful from here on. This isn't a walk in the park."

Before they went any further, Danny redistributed the weapons. He forced Ed, under protestation, to take the Colt belt and one of the pistols. The other he gave to Stefan who stuck it inside the wide belt around his waist.

"If anything comes at us, we don't hesitate," Danny said. Tommy's eyes were wide.

"Can I get a gun, Ed? Can I?"

Danny saw tears in Ed's eyes again, so he stepped forward to put a hand on Tommy's shoulder.

"Tell you what, lad, you look after Elsa for a while and maybe later I'll give you some lessons with the pistol. How does that sound?"

Tommy's smile was back full force again and as they moved back onto their downhill trail he took the lead, with Elsa at his heel as if she belonged there.

- 8 -

The Colt felt too awkward and heavy at Ed's hip, seeming to work against him with every step he took, the belt itself chafing at his waist. But better that he suffer some discomfort than putting the weapon back in Tommy's hand; in his current state, Tommy might do himself, or one of the others, a real mischief by accident.

The finding of the cairn and the knight's remains had shaken Ed to the core; he'd uncovered tangible evidence after all these months of hope, only to realise that the search for treasure was now of secondary import. It had created a dichotomy in his mind that he had yet to fully comprehend but all he had to do was look at Tommy ahead of them to firm up his resolve.

"I'm the big brother now," he muttered. "It's time I started acting like it and stopped feeling sorry for myself."

Stefan must have heard him.

"Do not berate yourself," he said. "It is no fault of yours that things took this turn. Never fear, Elsa will lead us out, we shall find the doctor for your brother, and shall all be back in the village for supper, you'll see."

Elsa had turned at the mention of her name, her tail wagging furiously.

"Home, Elsa," Stefan said. "Take us home."

The tail stopped wagging immediately and the dog whined deep in her throat. She started to come back up the slope towards them, then whined again, looked left and right then went back to Tommy's side, looking miserable.

"Home, Elsa," Stefan said, more forcibly this time.

The dog started walking back down the slope along the side of the stream, but some of the bounce had gone out of her step.

"She will see us home," Stefan said, but now he sounded as if he was trying too hard to convince himself of the fact.

They continued down the slope.

The cavern seemed endless. At times, the roof was a high vault, cathedral-like above them. At other points, it descended so low that the dangling roots brushed at the top of their heads and had Tommy complaining about cabbage again. And all the time the small stream gurgled away downhill beside them. Ed's gut was now telling him that they were indeed going in the wrong direction, but he could see no alternative to their current course.

Nobody had spoken for several minutes, each of them lost in their thoughts. At least the pains in Ed's chest wounds had eased, but that too served to remind him how long they had been in the cavern. He was about to speak up about the folly of going any deeper when Danny stopped.

"Do you feel that? There's a breeze."

He had just lit a cheroot and he held it up for them to see that the smoke was drifting in a definite wind that was coming from somewhere below. Elsa lifted her head, sniffed at the air, then barked once before bounding away down the slope. Tommy headed off after her with a yelp of his own.

"Tommy, come back," Ed shouted, but the youth and the dog were paying no heed, heading away now at some speed to where the roof dipped again and gloomy shadows gathered some two hundred yards away.

Ed broke into a run to go after them. He heard Danny and Stefan join him at his back but all his concentration was on watching his footing and trying to control the shifting weight of the pistol at his hip to avoid it tugging him off balance. Ahead of him his brother and the dog ducked under a very low-hanging outcrop of rock and disappeared from sight into the shadows beyond.

"Tommy!" Ed shouted, and put on a burst of speed he hadn't realised he possessed. Something tore at his chest, one of the bandages giving way under the stress. Blood trickled, warm against his belly inside his shirt. He paid it no heed. He almost caved his skull in by neglecting to duck in time when he reached the low outcrop, but he got away with no more than an abrasion on his forehead then he was out in a more open area again. Ahead of them was a rock wall with three caverns stretching away into blackness. Tommy stood at the mouth of the right hand one, tears streaming down his cheeks.

"He went in there," he said, pointing into the dark maw of the cave. "Tommy didn't follow. Tommy doesn't like the dark. It smells bad."

By this time, Stefan had arrived at Ed's side.

"Elsa, heel," he shouted.

The only sound was the men's labored breathing. Danny arrived to join them and all four of them stood at the cave entrance. Tommy was right, it smelled rank, a stench of rotting meat and musk.

"It's a predator's den," Danny said. "I've smelled this before."

"And I," Stefan said grimly. "But if Elsa is in there, I must go and get her."

Danny put a hand on the shepherd's shoulder, but it was brushed away.

"You cannot dissuade me, my friend. She would do the same for me."

"We have no light," Ed said. "We lost our lamps in the water."

Stefan went back to the low-hanging rock and gathered

clumps of root in his hands. When he stepped into the cave mouth, Ed saw that the vegetation gave off enough of a glow for them to see several feet ahead of them, but no more than that. The shepherd stepped forward.

"Wait," Danny called. "If you go, we all go. I won't have us splitting up the group…not when there might be a beastie of some sort about." He turned to Ed. "Gather up more of yon cabbage, lads. Let's give our shepherd some light."

A minute later, all four of them carried a bundle of roots, two-handed in front of them as they inched into the cave.

"Elsa," Stefan shouted, but there was only silence and darkness ahead of them. The stench was even more pronounced inside the cave and Ed took to breathing shallowly through his mouth to try to minimise the impact.

"It smells like shite," Tommy said, then giggled until Ed had to hush him. Then Ed had to pick up the pace to keep up with the shepherd, who was almost running now, his concern for the dog overcoming any fear.

"Elsa!" he shouted again, and this time got a whimpering yelp in reply.

They turned a corner, entered in a wider, higher, chamber that was dimly lit by more of the foliage, and discovered why the dog hadn't come at Stefan's command. She was on the far side of the chamber, lying flat on her stomach, her ears pinned back, lips pulled up and showing her teeth to the thing that almost filled the area between her and the newly arrived men.

Ed recognised it immediately as another of the wyrm-like things, similar to the one that had attacked him at the waterfall. But this one was larger, much larger. The thickest part of the body was broad and barrel-shaped, some two feet in diameter, supported by four legs like tree trunks capped with metal-like talons. The head, horse shaped as before, turned to stare at the approaching men to reveal a maw filled with sharp, pointed teeth between which a too-red tongue slithered. It lay in a coil in the center of the chamber, tail tucked away somewhere below it and it appeared to be confused by the presence of the four new arrivals in its domain.

"Is it a horse?" Tommy said at Ed's back, and that was the cue for the thing to move. It opened its mouth and hissed, spraying all four of the men with fine spittle that tasted as foul as anything they'd smelled so far. Ed hadn't even considered going for his pistol, such had been his shock at seeing the beast, but both Danny and Stefan had no such qualms. Ed got pushed none too softly aside as Danny stepped forward. He put two shots down its throat and Stefan put out one of the great red eyes for good measure.

"Why didn't it attack us?" Ed said as the beast slumped in on itself. At the movement, something underneath it squirmed and squealed. Elsa finally moved, leaping forward and, as if she'd caught a rabbit or rat, grabbed at something white and wriggling, shaking it violently from side to side until it went limp. Beneath the body of the wyrm something else squealed. Elsa dropped the thing she had in her jaws. She lunged again, but this time she came to heel when Stefan called her. Danny went forward first and looked down inside the coiled girth of the dead beast. He sucked at his teeth and motioned Ed and Stefan forward, pointing down to where five white writhing bodies lay, young wyrm, not long birthed, with a sixth lying dead where Elsa had dropped it.

"There's why she didn't attack," Danny said. "She was protecting her brood."

"Baby horses?" Tommy said from behind them. "Can I see?"

"No," Ed said, sharper than he intended. "Stay back, Tommy. It's not safe."

He turned back to see Danny raise his pistol and aim downward.

"No, you can't."

"We have to," Stefan said, raising his own gun. "It's a mercy. With the mother dead, they won't survive in any case."

Ed led Tommy away as the sound of pistol shots echoed loudly around them. He thought that Tommy might be crying again, but couldn't tell, for his own eyes had suddenly misted over.

- 9 -

Danny strode out of the cave and took a deep, welcome, gulp of fresher air. It had been grisly work and although as Stefan had said it was a mercy killing, he still felt as if he'd just shot a puppy. His ears still rang from the pistol fire, like church bells in his head, and his guts were roiling from both the tension and the stench in the cave. He felt mightily relieved to be out of it. Ed and Tommy were standing in the cave mouth, both of them looking as miserable as Danny felt. Even Elsa seemed subdued as she came out at Stefan's heel.

"Quickly now," Danny said, his voice sounding distant and echoing in his ears. "We need to get away from here, as far as we can as fast as we can."

Stefan nodded in understanding, but Ed was slower on the uptake.

"I thought that we might have a rest?"

"Not here. Where there's a mother and a brood, there's a

father. I'm guessing it was he who killed yon horse-thing back up the trail. We don't want to be meeting him. He might be an angry beastie when he sees what we've just done. No, we move, and we move fast."

The stream they had been following descended sharply here, heading down into a steep-walled gully. As Danny led them towards it, he noted again the breeze in his face. It was coming up out of the gully.

"It's going to carry our scent back into the cavern but that can't be helped. Come on, lads. Where there's wind, there's generally open air. We can't be far from an exit back to the world. And the sooner we get there, the happier I shall be."

Danny went first into the gully. He'd reholstered his pistol but his hand rarely stayed far from it.

The gully narrowed almost as soon as they entered it, necessitating that they travel single file. Danny went first with the brothers in the middle and Stefan and Elsa bringing up the rear.

The breeze was stronger now, full in his face and doing much to dispel the odor of the beasts' den from his nose and throat. What it couldn't do was wash the memory from his mind; the mother had been huge, twelve feet in length, maybe more.

And if she's that big, what about the male?

He hadn't mentioned it to the others as he didn't want to frighten either of the brothers, but he'd had occasion to beard a lioness in a den in Africa. On that occasion, he'd also been party to the killing of cubs…and suffered the consequences when they met a big, maned male on leaving the den. He'd lost a good friend that day, mainly due to youthful overconfidence. He wasn't about to make the same mistake again.

The gully narrowed further. They were now walking in the stream, rushing water lapping at their ankles. The vertical walls on either side were almost close enough to touch, and it was darker here, the illuminating roots hanging from a roof that was fifty yards and more above them.

The first indication that they were in trouble came when a bellowing roar echoed down the gully from somewhere behind them, a howl every bit as terrifying as any lion in rage.

"Faster," Danny shouted, and without waiting to see if anyone obeyed him he put on a burst of speed, throwing caution to the wind in a dangerous descent over wet rocks. He knew that at any step his footing might betray him and that a single slip might lead to a broken leg, which would surely be fatal in their current circumstances. But if that howl had come from the beast he was imagining in his mind, he didn't want to meet it here in this narrow gully; it would be bloody carnage.

The descent became a nightmare of splashing water, thudding feet and frenzied howling from behind them that was getting increasingly loud as the gully narrowed even further, so much so that at points Danny had to turn almost side on to squeeze through the passageway. He had been looking down, checking ahead for sure footing, but now chanced a look up, checking if the passage might show signs of reaching an end and a more open area where they might make a stand side by side. But there was only gloom and darker shadows below.

Finally, the howling got too loud behind them to ignore. It was either turn and face it or be chased down like a rabbit in a burrow with the hounds at his heels. Danny turned and drew his pistol in a single smooth movement.

"Get down," he shouted. "Get down at my side, and cover me if you can."

Stefan moved quickly to comply, but Ed couldn't get Tommy to move. The older brother seemed stuck to the spot, the fear big in his eyes as the wild howls screamed around them.

"What is it, Eddie? What is it?"

"Quiet, Tommy. Come on, get down here with me. Danny's going to look after us."

"I want my mum," Tommy wailed and as if in reply, another bellow came from their back.

Then Danny saw it, a lighter shape against the dark rock, slithering down the gully towards them like some great cave-snake. It was even larger than he'd imagined, fifteen feet and more from snout to tail, most of it muscle, at least the bits that weren't teeth and talons. At the same time he saw it, it saw them and as if given new impetus in barreled down the gully towards them, as fast as if it was dropping from a great height.

"Down," Danny shouted, raising his pistol, but still Tommy wouldn't cooperate. Danny saw Ed trying to manhandle his brother to the ground, but knew it was going to be too late; the brothers were blocking his line of sight for a clear shot, and the beast, howling its triumph, was almost on them.

They got a second's respite when the beast was forced to take pause and squeeze its bulk through one of the narrower parts of the passageway. That allowed Danny time to lean to one side and attempt to take aim past the brothers, but it was going to be a risky shot to take. He was aware that Stefan was down at his left side, pistol raised, but the shepherd's aim was even more impeded than Danny's, the brothers' bodies between him and the beast.

Danny was still calculating the risks of taking a shot when Elsa took the matter out of his hands. The dog let out a howl almost as loud as that of the beast and launched herself away from Stefan, past the brothers and into the face of the beast. Stefan moved to go after her but Danny held him down with his spare hand; he'd seen what Stefan hadn't. The dog's attack had finally broken Tommy's immobility, but instead of moving to safety, the youth turned and stepped forward towards where Elsa was trying to avoid the wyrm's slavering jaws, looking for an opening to get at its throat.

The next few seconds seemed to pass in slow motion and with a sense of inevitable doom. Tommy bent to try to drag the dog away from the wyrm but only succeeded in bringing himself inside the reach of its front left foot. A talon raked across Tommy's shin, opening his leg to the bone. Blood flew in an arc across the worm's snout, enraging it all the more. It made a lunge with its jaws for the wounded leg. That gave Elsa the opening she'd been looking for. The dog leapt forward and attached itself to the wyrm's throat. Danny's line of sight cleared as Tommy fell to one side, yelling in pain and misery. He fired, but the wyrm had moved too quickly, thrashing its head to one side and throwing Elsa against the gully wall with a sickening thud. A second shot, which Danny knew had to come from Stefan, raised a bloody red furrow along the wyrm's snout. The sound of the shot and the sudden pain seemed to confuse the beast. It paused any attack long enough for Danny to take aim again. He tried for one of the egg-sized red eyes but again the beast moved at just the wrong time and he hit what must have been a bony ridge above the eye socket, leaving little more than a bloody scratch.

It was enough though; the beast retreated in the face of the pistols, scrambling away almost as fast as it had come. Danny sent two more shots after it, unsure in the gloom if he had hit anything. Elsa struggled to her feet, went to run after the departing beast, then yelped in pain before going still.

"Danny," Ed called out. "I can't stop the bleeding. He's hurt bad."

"Stefan," Danny said. "Watch our back. It could return at any moment."

He didn't waste any time checking that the shepherd had complied. He bent to where Tommy sat, back to the gully wall, blood oozing from a wound that had opened his shin from just below the kneecap all the way down to the top of his foot, bone showing amid the blood. Tommy had his eyes firmly closed, refusing to look at his leg, and he was obviously stifling yelps of pain every time Ed tried to get close to it.

"Tourniquet," Danny said. "Your belt, quick now, lad, before he bleeds out entirely."

Tommy's face had taken on an almost gray pallor that Danny didn't like at all, and as Danny applied then tightened the makeshift tourniquet at the lad's thigh, there was only a flickering of his eyelids to show that he'd taken any notice of the procedure.

"He's going to be okay," Ed said, almost to himself. "We can fix him up."

Danny didn't reply. Experience told him the lad's odds were at best fifty-fifty, and that would have been in a place with access to modern medicine. Here in the damp dark, with no escape looking imminent, he couldn't speak his conclusions out loud; the younger brother wasn't ready to hear them. Rather than face the agony he knew he'd see in Ed's eyes, he turned away to see Stefan bent over the dog.

"How is she?"

"A broken rib, possibly," the shepherd replied. "But there's no blood in her mouth; I don't think she's punctured anywhere."

As if to prove her health the dog wagged her tail twice and walked in a tight circle, unsteadily at first then with more confidence.

"Good," Danny replied. "She can get along on her own. It'll need the three of us to get Tommy here on the move. We need to find somewhere we can shelter and keep him warm; he's lost too much blood."

Stefan had a long look at the sitting lad then turned back to Danny. It was obvious he'd reached the same conclusion as Danny had. Danny saw the question coming and put a finger to his lips to warn the shepherd that Ed would be listening. Stefan was quick enough on the uptake to answer with a small nod.

"Ed," Danny said. "Help me get him up. We need to find shelter, somewhere we can defend where we can keep Tommy warm."

Ed looked up through fresh tears.

"It wasn't supposed to be like this."

Danny could have told him that those same words could have been heard from soldiers the world over at any minute of the day, but held his peace as he bent to help with getting the wounded lad on his feet.

Tommy was a dead weight, lost either in sleep or

unconsciousness; either way, Danny thought it to be a blessing, for there would only be a world of pain waiting for him on waking.

They carried him between them as well as they were able, heading down the gully. Every two steps Danny looked back, expecting to see an onrushing beast at any moment. But no attack came and after several minutes of descent, the gully showed signs of opening out into a bigger chamber. Several caves dotted the sides and the third they reached proved to be big enough, dry enough and deep enough to accommodate all of them and give them a clear view of the gully such that they would see any attack coming.

"I'll see what I can gather that we can burn," Danny said as they laid Tommy against the far wall. The lad was still out, his eyes fluttering wildly behind his lids, but at least the tourniquet was doing its job and there was only a small amount of blood seeping from the wound.

"Release the pressure on the belt a bit," Danny told Stefan. "If I'm not back in five minutes, you should get on the move, get the lads out of here as best you can."

Again, all he got in return from the shepherd was a nod, but he didn't need anything else. With one hand on his pistol and the other on the hilt of his saber, Danny headed out in search of firewood.

Elsa trotted beside him at his heel.

- 10 -

Ed forced himself to watch as Stefan released the pressure on the tourniquet and fresh blood oozed blackly from Tommy's wound.

"We should bandage him up," Ed said. "Shouldn't we?"

Stefan shook his head.

"Let it bleed a bit. You never can tell with animal wounds." The shepherd produced a canteen from his bag and began carefully washing Tommy's leg. At the sight of the gaping flaps of skin, Ed had to turn away, his guts roiling.

For the first time since their hurried arrival, he took in details of the cave. The roof was some six feet overhead, a sparse cover of hanging roots providing a dim light. The cave itself was twenty feet or so in depth, half again as wide at the mouth and tapering at the end where Tommy was propped against the wall. The mouth was three good steps up from the bed of the gully and away from the flowing water so was dry inside, and there was, thankfully, no sign that any animal had ever made a den there. Their view was only of the opposite wall of the gully. Ed was about to step into the mouth to check on Danny when Stefan called from the rear.

"He's coming round."

Stefan came to the cave mouth and swapped places with Ed. As Ed turned, he saw that Stefan already had the pistol in his hand; Ed had been standing in open view, the pistol still in its holster. Had the beast attacked, he would have been powerless against it. He knew intellectually that he had to get a grip on the situation, for Tommy's sake if nothing else, but a fog of fear had him held tight and he was having trouble clearing it from his mind. A moan from Tommy got him moving and he hurried to the rear of the cave.

Tommy's face looked far too white in the gloom, smooth as a piece of fine porcelain except for a puffed redness around the eyes where tears still flowed.

"It hurts, Eddie," he said in little more than a whisper. "It hurts so bad."

Ed saw that the shepherd's bag lay at Tommy's side. A delve inside came up with the brandy flask, a shake of which showed there still to be some liquor inside. He put it to Tommy's lips and got an immediate reaction.

"I don't like that," Tommy said. "It smells bad. Like Dad

when he's angry."

That almost brought tears to Ed's eyes again, but he managed to hold them back.

"It makes Dad sleepy too, doesn't it? You remember that, don't you, Tommy?"

Tommy nodded, reluctantly, eyeing the flask warily.

"Just a few sips, Tommy. Come on, for me. It'll take the hurt away."

"You promise? Cross your heart?"

"And hope to die…" Ed said, and suddenly the tears were uncontainable, flowing down his cheeks even as Tommy took several long gulps from the brandy flask. The liquor almost choked him, bringing two coughs, but he kept it all down, all the time staring Ed in the eyes; Ed realised he was deliberately not looking at the wound.

"You'll look after me, Eddie, won't you? You wouldn't leave me here in the dark?"

"Nobody's leaving anybody," Ed said. "You rest now, Tommy. Have a sleep, and when you wake up, we'll be on our way home."

"That sounds nice," Tommy said, but now his voice was so weak as to be almost inaudible. His eyes closed and his head slumped forward onto his chest. For a panicked minute, Ed thought he'd gone, but putting his head down next to Tommy's he was able to hear a labored hiss and gurgle of shallow, rapid breathing, and on testing for a pulse he felt his brother's heart racing at his wrist.

"It's best if he sleeps," Stefan said from the cave mouth. "But we need to keep a close eye on him."

The shepherd sounded grave, and Ed was reluctant to question him, for he knew in his heart he would not relish the answer. He made sure Tommy was fully asleep then went to the entrance to join the shepherd.

"It's bad, isn't it?" he said.

Stefan nodded.

"You have to prepare yourself, lad. Your brother may die before we leave this cave. It's in the Lord's hands now."

"We can bandage him up, get him walking, and…"

"Walking on that wound isn't an option. It would bleed too much and he'd be gone all the sooner."

"Then what do we do?"

"We wait. If he wakes up, we will see about that bandage."

Ed didn't like the sound of that "if."

He didn't like it at all.

Further conversation was curtailed when Danny arrived back. He carried two armfuls of dried roots and dumped them unceremoniously at Ed's feet. Elsa came along behind him, looking very pleased with herself as she dropped the carcass of one of the rabbit-things beside the firewood.

"There's another cavern down the slope," Danny said. "A big one. More firewood and more of the rabbits there too. Get a fire going. We'll be back."

Without another word, he'd turned away again, and again Elsa followed close at his heel.

For the next few minutes, Ed managed to concentrate enough to, with the help of Stefan's flint and tinder, get the fire going while the shepherd went out to the gully to gut and clean the rabbit in the water. Stefan made up a rudimentary spit and by the time Danny returned with another load of wood, the rabbit was cooking over a well-established fire.

"The breeze is going to take the smell back up the shaft," Danny said, frowning. "But that can't be helped. The beastie already knows where we are if it wants us. Let's just hope we gave it enough of a fright to keep it at bay for a while."

"It did not look particularly afraid to me, my friend," Stefan said, and Danny laughed grimly.

"Nor to me. But it has not returned as of yet. We must take good signs where we can find them."

Ed was only half-listening. Most of his attention was on Tommy. He had to stop himself from going back to the rear of the cave again; it had only been a minute since he'd last checked for signs of breathing. Danny saw his agitation.

"Let him sleep, lad. That's all we can do for him just now."

"He should eat," Ed protested.

"We'll save him some. Sleep and warmth, and time. Especially time."

"Does he have enough blood left in him to give him that time?"

Danny didn't answer but Ed had seen his eyes before he turned away. A wash of helplessness in the face of Tommy's predicament came over him, and again the tears flowed. Elsa took note and came to Ed's side, offering herself for petting and companionship and for a time, she helped his state of mind. But his gaze kept turning to the rear of the cave, and the tears were never far off.

Danny made two more forays for wood, and Elsa went with him the second time, once again returning with a rabbit.

"You say there's a larger cavern below?" Stefan asked.

"Aye," Danny replied. "The breeze is stronger there too. Mayhap we are getting closer to an exit. When the lad wakes, we shall see what can be done about making our escape."

Ed had a feeling that last sentence had been for his benefit, an attempt to raise his spirits. He wasn't sure anything was capable of doing that at that moment. He had no appetite, ending up feeding most of his share of the rabbits to Elsa, who seemed none the worse for wear for her encounter with the beast. The same could not be said for Tommy.

The older brother was still asleep, slumped on the ground

right at the rear of the cave, which was rapidly warming as the hot air from the fire circulated. His breathing was now punctuated with moans, high wails that seemed to come from deep in his chest, and every one of them tore at Ed's heart.

"We need to do something for him," he said, addressing Danny. The old soldier had stood away from the fire and was at the mouth of the cave smoking a cheroot. When he turned back his face was in shadow, but his speech was grave.

"It's out of our hands, lad. Either he lives or he dies, and either way it's not up to us."

"But the wound. We should at least bandage it…"

"It wouldn't do much good," Danny replied, echoing Stefan from earlier. "And here's another thing you don't want to hear. We may have to amputate."

That knocked all the wind out of Ed, the word and the thought of it almost too large for his mind to hold.

"Take his leg? No. I won't allow it."

"We might not have a choice. Animal wounds can fester fast if not tended properly. I've seen strong men taken in a matter of hours. And your brother is currently not a strong man."

"I won't allow it," Ed said, softly, almost to himself, just as another of Tommy's moans echoed around them.

- 11 -

If anything, Danny thought he'd gone too easy on young Ed. He'd gone to the rear of the cave just five minutes previously to relieve some of the pressure on the tourniquet, and the leg had taken on that grey, bloated look that Danny had seen too many times on battlefields thousands of miles from this hole in the deep. But Africa, India, or here, the outcome was likely to be the same. Without a doctor, the lad was more likely to die than live.

"We should leave this place," Stefan said from his seat by the fire. "It feels wrong."

"That it does, my friend, that it does. We'll give the lad another hour then we'll see about moving him."

"We will not be able to carry him far," the shepherd said, keeping his voice low so that Ed, who had moved to the rear of the cave again, would not hear.

"I know," Danny replied. "But we may be able to rig up some

kind of litter; there is more vegetation and dried root strewn in the next chamber. With that and the rope, we should be able to get something made to lie him on. I am more worried about corruption."

"I heard you mention amputation to the young one. Do you have experience of performing this procedure?"

"Once, on the battlefield," Danny replied, remembering the blood and screams. He patted his sabre. "We have the blade, we have a fire to cauterize it quickly. I think I could get the job done swiftly. But then we'd need to get him to a doctor fast. It would depend on how quickly we can get out of here."

Stefan didn't reply to that. He didn't have to; both of them knew the odds were stacked high against them. There were just too many things that could go wrong and too many that needed to go exactly right.

And we haven't been doing very well on those so far.

The decision was taken out of their hands some time later.

Tommy woke and immediately began to scream, his howls as loud as those of the wyrm had been earlier.

"Oh, God, Eddie. It hurts. It hurts so bad."

Danny was at Ed's shoulder as they went to Tommy's side, and they saw the state of the wound at the same time. It looked almost as if someone had frothed-up soap and applied it to the leg; a white scum bubbled the whole length of the cut from knee to ankle.

"Bloody poison," Danny muttered, and turned to Ed.

"Can you hold him? It's going to have to come off."

Ed's eyes were still fixed on the wound, and he didn't reply until Danny shook him by the shoulder.

"Lad, can you hold him?" he said more urgently. "Otherwise, fetch the shepherd. This has to be done now. Even then, if it's in his blood, we may be too late."

"What's he talking about, Eddie?" Tommy wailed, but Danny ignored him. He drew his saber, returned to the fire and plunged the blade into the center of it, leaving it there for a count of twenty before removing it and striding back to the rear of the cave.

"Hold him," he said, his voice carrying enough command for Ed to finally move. Tommy's eyes went big when he saw the sword, and he thrashed in Ed's arms.

"Hold him still, for pity's sake. This has to be done swiftly if it is to be done at all."

Danny steeled his resolve and focused on the leg, trying not to think of it as something attached to a human being, trying to make himself believe it was as simple as chopping wood.

The blade went up, came down, Tommy howled, Elsa wailed in sympathy, and Danny looked down in horror to see that the job had been botched; he'd only managed to partially sever the leg at the kneecap. Tommy thrashed like a wild beast and it was all Ed could do to hold him down. Even despite the tourniquet, blood flew in an arc that splashed the cave wall.

"Damnit, lad," Danny shouted. "Hold him bloody still or it'll be your leg that I take next."

The roar of fury from the old soldier stunned both younger men into temporary silence which Danny took advantage of at once. A second strike with the saber finally did the trick. The bottom half of the leg fell away. Tommy wailed at the sight, then his eyes rolled up in their sockets and he fell into Ed's arms, a dead weight.

"Tighten the tourniquet," Danny said to Ed. "We have a matter of seconds now."

He strode back to the fire, retrieved a stretch of root that was only burning at one end, and quickly returned to the stricken youth. He applied the burning end to the stump, forcing himself to hold it there even as the skin turned black and the stench of burnt meat filled the cave.

"At least he wasn't awake to suffer that," Danny muttered. "A small blessing."

He tossed the root away and bent to Tommy's side. For a terrible few seconds, he thought that the shock had already killed him, then he felt for a pulse and found one, thin and fast but there. He checked the eyes, finding that they were still rolled up in the sockets, eyelids fluttering.

Ed sat to one side, his face pale. He was still staring at the severed portion of Tommy's leg. Danny kicked it away into a dark corner and grabbed Ed by the shoulders, looking him in the eyes.

"Come on, lad. That's the worst of it done. Get your head into the present. Your brother needs you more than ever."

That appeal to duty did the trick. Ed's gaze focused, seemed to realize where he was, and the youth nodded.

"What do we do now?"

"I think we should move, while he's asleep. We need to get him to a doctor, and we need to do it soon."

Stefan was already kicking out the fire and gathering up their belongings as Danny and Ed struggled to get the dead weight of the unconscious Tommy upright.

"At least he's lighter now," Ed said, and laughed, a high, frightened thing that spoke of near madness.

"Steady, lad," Danny said. "Remember, you're all he's got."

Finally, they got Tommy steadied between them. He did indeed feel lighter, much lighter, as if there was little more than a wisp of him left. As they started to walk out of the cave, Ed turned back.

"His leg…"

"Do you want to carry it?" Danny said, rather more harshly than he'd intended. He softened his voice. "It's of no use to him now, lad. Leave it be."

With Stefan and Elsa taking the lead, the small band made their way out of the cave and turned to head down the slope.

As if aware that its prey was once more out in the open, the great wyrm howled somewhere high above at their backs.

"Just keep going down," Danny said when Stefan turned to
ask for directions. "It opens out in twenty yards or so, as I said, a
bigger cavern. We'll see about getting a litter made for the lad
there."

They reached the opening and looked over a wider cavern.
Like the others, this too was lit by the hanging, luminescent roots,
but here the vegetation on the cavern floor was more vigorous and
more varied than they'd previously seen. Larger bushes, almost
trees punctuated the landscape, interspersed by large patches of
wispy, pale grasses. In the distance, several hundred yards down
the slope, Danny saw a herd of a score and more of the horse-like
things and the sound of furtive scurrying in the grass told him that
there were more of the rabbits for Elsa to hunt if need be.

"Put him down, lad," he said to Ed. "Gently now. Let's see if
we can get a litter made for him; it'll be easier going dragging him
rather than carrying him."

Ed did as he was bid and they laid Tommy out on a soft patch
of grass, then Danny left Stefan on guard duty as he went to
forage.

Once again, Elsa followed at his heel.

- 12 -

Ed couldn't shift his gaze from the blackened stump and the empty space below it where his brother's leg used to be.

"We shouldn't have left it behind," he said, more to himself than anything else, but Stefan heard.

"Left what behind?"

"The leg. What if that wyrm should come upon it and eat it?"

Stefan laughed bitterly.

"Then we will have fed it, and mayhap it will leave us alone. It is only a leg, young sir. Be thankful that is all that is lost."

Tommy was still out cold, whether unconscious or simply asleep, Ed found it impossible to tell. Either way, he was somewhere where the pain couldn't reach him; there was that at least to be thankful for.

Stefan passed him a lit cigarette and Ed smoked it down without really noticing it. He saw Danny farther down the slope, his arms already full of pieces of dry wood and vegetation.

"I should go and help," Ed said, but Stefan held him back.

"You watch your brother, I watch the two of you, and Elsa watches her new friend. That is the way it is to be. Understand?"

Ed understood well enough. He didn't have to like it though, but just then Tommy let out a moan and Ed was at his side again in seconds.

There was pain in Tommy's eyes when he looked up, but also surprise.

"Ed? Where are we?"

The little lost boy voice was gone; older Tommy had resurfaced. But it appeared he had no memory of anything since bashing his head coming down the water chute from above.

"What is this place?" he said, tried to sit up…and noticed the empty space where his leg had been. He screamed, a wail that echoed around the whole cavern. There was an answering howl, far off back the way they had come, thankfully distant. But Ed's attention now was on his brother. He held Tommy down, put his head close to his brother's face and began explaining, slowly and carefully, trying to ensure he understood. Tommy was in no mood to listen.

"You took my bloody leg off," Tommy shouted. He was looking over Ed's shoulder at where Danny was returning.

"It was either that or let you die," Danny said, as casually as if he were passing the time of day in the street. "You're welcome, by the way."

Ed had turned to look at Danny, so he only caught Tommy's movement out of the corner of his eye just as he felt the pistol leave the holster at his hip. When he turned round, Tommy had the weapon raised, pointing at Danny.

"You bastard," Tommy said. His aim wavered alarmingly; the pistol was obviously too heavy for him in his weakened state, but the redness at his cheeks showed that it was rage that was fueling him at present.

Danny dropped the wood at his feet and stood, relaxed and easy with his hand falling naturally over the grip of his own pistol.

"Put that away, lad, before you do someone a mischief."

"We had to do it," Ed said. "You were poisoned."

"We? You were in on it too?" Tommy said, swing the pistol to aim it at Ed's chest. "My own brother?"

Tommy was shouting again, and again it was answered by a screaming howl from above. It sounded closer now, and as if for the first time Tommy took note of it.

"What in blazes is that?"

"That, my lad," Danny said, "is the thing you should be angry at. It was yon bogle that gave you the wound that led to us doing what had to be done."

The old soldier had his pistol in his hand now; Ed hadn't seen him draw it, and neither had Tommy, who was now looking Ed in the eye.

"What's he talking about? What bogle? What wound?"

Finally, Tommy's strength gave out and he couldn't hold the pistol any longer. It fell with a soft thud to the grass where Ed grabbed it and tossed it back towards Danny. Tommy fell backwards, utterly spent. The color had gone from his cheeks again, leaving him as pale as alabaster, and his eyelids fluttered weakly.

"Bastards," he whispered faintly, then was out again, his breathing rapid and shallow. When Ed felt for a pulse, it was to find it racing even faster than before.

"Do me a favor, lad," Danny said laconically. "Keep him away from the guns...or anything sharp for that matter. I don't think he's in the best frame of mind."

The howling rose again in the cavern they had left behind.

"It is getting closer," Stefan said.

"I know," Danny replied. He nodded towards the pile of wood and vegetation. "Give me a hand with this, would you? Some of the wood looks fibrous. We've got rope, and something to tie it up with. We should be able to make a litter."

He turned back to Ed.

"Watch your brother. And mind what I said about weapons."

Ed felt like a spare wheel as he watched the other two men

build the litter. They worked calmly and efficiently, as if they'd been a team for years. Elsa lay at Stefan's side. She showed no interest in Tommy now, obviously preferring the boy that had been to the man now returned.

In some ways, Ed knew how the dog felt. There had been an innocence and charm there that Ed had missed in the intervening years. Tommy had grown into a hard-hearted, self-centered young man, and if they hadn't been brothers, Ed might not want anything to do with him. And yet, looking at him now, helpless, maimed, possibly dying, it was impossible not to feel the tug of old filial strings.

"I promised to look after you, Tommy," he whispered. "That's one vow I'll not break, no matter how angry you get."

It only took a matter of minutes for Danny and Stefan to put a rudimentary litter together from wood, rope, leafy vegetation from the bushy scrubs, and makeshift cords fashioned from strips of fibrous bark. Danny looked at it critically.

"It'll hold, for a while at least. It'll probably need two of us at a time to shift it though, which means only one gun on guard. I don't like it."

Ed didn't like it either. The wounds at his chest were far from healed, he was already as tired as he'd ever felt in his life, and now he was going to be asked to help haul the dead weight of his brother across rough terrain with a wild beast howling somewhere at his back.

What's not to like?

But when Danny gave the order to move out, Ed moved.

He owed it to his brother. He owed it to himself.

He didn't take the pistol when Danny offered to return it.

"I don't trust Tommy," he said sadly. "And I don't trust myself not to give in to him."

He undid the belt and holster and passed them to Stefan who looked like a pirate in his shepherd's clothes with the pair of Colts strapped to his hips. He took up the extended pole at one side of the litter, Stefan took the other, and, after an initial heave to get the thing moving, were soon walking, albeit slowly, down the slope.

Danny and Elsa brought up the rear.

- 13 -

To begin with, they made good time over what proved to be even ground, almost pasture-like. The stone ceiling was high above their heads now and a stiff breeze in Danny's face made the cavern feel somehow more open, less oppressive.

Ahead of him, young Ed and Stefan seemed to be handling the litter easily enough and with little discomfort and Tommy, thankfully, was still out for the count. Danny hoped that Ed didn't realise just how close his brother had been to getting himself shot; Danny had considered it, and if the lad hadn't dropped the gun when he did, he might well have acted on the impulse, brother or no brother.

He was watching Tommy for signs of consciousness when Elsa let out a yip at his side.

"What is it, girl?" he said, turning to look back up their trail, half-expecting to see the wyrm coming across the open ground towards them. But there was no sign of the beast, and when he looked down, he saw that the dog was looking, not backwards, but upwards towards their rocky ceiling.

At first, he wasn't sure what he was looking at, thinking it was merely a group of thicker, almost barrel-like roots dangling in a cluster. Then one opened out, flower-like, stretching a pair of pale, leathery wings that must have been almost ten feet in span and he realised it was a colony of bats…or at least, bat-like creatures. Like the rabbit and horse-things, these too had six limbs, two each of arms, legs, and wings. Their heads seemed to share the horse-like aspect of the Wyrm and their necks looked misshapen, too long for their bodies. The creatures hung upside down, clinging to the rock and roots with long-toed, clawed feet.

The one that had opened its wings closed them again, wrapping the leathery cloak around itself as it snuggled back into the tight group. Elsa barked again, a small yip only, as if afraid to bring attention to them.

"It's okay, girl," Danny said. "As long as they're up there, they're not down here. Live and let live, that's my motto."

All the same, he kept a close eye on the beasts as they passed underneath them and only breathed more easily when they'd passed the spot and the bats were some way behind them.

They were still following the same stream that had been their trail from the beginning but now it meandered slowly across an almost flat plain, the slope having leveled out. The cavern they were in appeared endless, its far end obscured in gloomy shadows. The horse-things, having been spooked on their approach, had retreated off somewhere to Danny's left out of sight behind a copse of thicker gorse and now the group of men were the only things moving in the stillness of the cavern.

Silence fell, the only sound the scuffing of the rear of the litter across the dry vegetation underfoot. It was broken by Tommy as the litter bounced over an unseen rock, shaking the whole frame and bringing him awake with a start and a howl of pain. The howl was answered from their rear by the wail of the wyrm and this time when Danny turned, it was to see the pale beast come barreling out of the gully, heading at a run across the plain towards them.

Stefan dropped his end of the litter and made to draw the pistols but Danny stopped him with a shout.

"No, not here in the open; he'll run over us like a train even if we get some shots into him. We don't have the firepower. Run!"

He pointed to his left to the thick copse of gorse.

"In there if we can, and hope it slows him down."

Stefan took up the pole again and they ran. Every step caused the litter to bounce, bringing howls of pain from Tommy and wild screams of anticipation from the approaching wyrm.

They splashed through the thankfully shallow stream and reached the copse not more than thirty yards ahead of the thundering beast.

Danny stopped at the edge of the gorse and turned, drawing both his pistol and his sword although he thought neither would prove much use; he was merely trying to gain time for the others to get under cover. He heard Tommy scream again behind him as Stefan and Ed forced the litter none too gently into the dense foliage, but Danny couldn't afford the time to turn around. With Elsa baring her teeth at his side, he raised his weapons and waited for the beast to come for him.

He knew he might only be given time for one shot. He took aim at a huge eye blazing in fury and pulled the trigger just as there was a snap, as of a sail in a wind, and a bat creature fell on the wyrm like a falcon taking a pigeon. His shot went high and wide. The pale thing's headlong rush came to a halt mere yards from where Danny stood but its attention was no longer on the men; two more of the bats dropped down and began to tear gouges in the beast's flanks, using talons both on their feet and on their small, almost withered, arms. All of the howling was now coming from the wyrm as the silent bats pressed another attack. The wyrm rolled and tumbled. Danny heard a crack as the spine of one of the bats broke and when the wyrm stood upright again, there was a dead bat beneath it. But more, a dozen and more, were already swooping out of the sky.

The wyrm turned tail and fled, harried all the way back to the gully by swooping bats.

Like crows seeing off an eagle, Danny thought, and realised the comparison was probably an apt one; it seemed that this particular cavern belonged to the bats and they didn't take kindly to a predator entering their domain.

Danny waited until the wyrm made a hasty retreat back up the gully in the distance and the bats whirled away to circle near the roof. Only when he was satisfied that another attack wasn't imminent did he turn to the gorse.

There was no sign of the others, but Elsa seemed to know where she was going. She made her way quickly through a gap in the foliage and Danny went through after her to find the others in a natural hiding spot, a hemispherical empty area where the gorse had grown out and then died away in the center. It was dim in the enclosed space but he saw that it was tall enough that they could stand upright and wide enough to accommodate all of them lying down if need be.

Stefan stood, pistols in hand and ready for action. Ed was tending to Tommy who lay flat on his back, whimpering, his face showing too white in the gloom.

"Brandy, for pity's sake, give him the brandy," Ed said.

Stephan shook his head.

"It is all gone, young sir. I have no more."

Ed turned to speak to Danny.

"What can we do? What can I do?"

There was nothing Danny could say that would be of any use. Instead, he addressed Stefan.

"It appears you've found us a hidey hole, for now at least. The bats should keep the big beastie away, and they don't seem to be interested in us. We should rest before moving on. Shall we say an hour?"

"We can't move him again," Ed said, almost shouting. "Can't you see the pain we are causing him?"

"There are two alternatives," Danny said. "We either wait here with him until he dies, or we leave him here to die alone while we go on. Which would you prefer?"

Ed reacted as if he'd been slapped.

"Leave him? You can't be serious?"

"What I'm seriously suggesting is that we rest for an hour and then move on as before with the litter. You are the one arguing against that."

Ed ran a hand through his hair.

"I'm sorry, it's just…"

Danny put a hand on his shoulder.

"Don't sweat it, lad. Look to your brother. That's all you can do."

Danny turned away, bent, and went out into the open again. The bats still circled high overhead but they were showing little interest in the men's position, and there was no sign of the wyrm.

When he went back under the canopy, Tommy was sitting up and having an earnest talk with his brother under his voice, almost whispering. He looked about as ill as anyone Danny had ever seen and still be alive.

"Brother stuff," Stefan said. He passed Danny a cigarette and they both lit up. Danny was grateful for the comfort the habit brought, a small piece of normality in what had turned into a madhouse.

"It is bad, no?" Stefan said.

"It is bad, yes," Danny replied. "But that breeze is stronger here. We could be getting close to an exit."

The look he got in return from Stefan told him that the shepherd wasn't sure of that conclusion.

"My belly is still telling me that we are going the wrong way," Stefan said.

Danny shrugged.

"It's the only way there is."

- 14 -

"Listen to me, Eddie," Tommy said. "You know I don't like the old soldier but he might have a point. You'll get out of this much easier without me."

"Don't you dare even consider it," Ed replied. "We're going home, both of us. Then we'll see how a one-legged man gets on in an arse-kicking contest."

Tommy tried to laugh but instead brought on a coughing fit that left him panting for breath before he could speak again.

"I can't do much more travelling on that," he said, nodding towards the litter. "Every step is like someone running a hot poker through what's left of my leg. It'll kill me."

"You'll die if we don't get you out of here."

Tommy reached for Ed's hand, turned it over to look at the gold ring.

"At least I'll go having seen that you were right all along."

Tommy's skin had taken on the same grey, wet sheen that had only been apparent on his leg earlier, with sweat running in rivulets from his hairline. His tongue was a dry, almost rock-like thing behind cracked, almost black lips. His eyes were sunk down in dark hollows, pupils dilated, giving him a maniacal stare. Where his fingers touched Ed's, they gave off heat as if being too close to a boiling pan. There were fresh tears among the sweat when he looked back into Ed's eyes.

"I've had it, Eddie, and we both know it."

"I know no such thing..."

Tommy cut him off.

"Look at me, Eddie. Look at me and see the truth, the way you saw it when you found that map."

For the first time since the amputation, Ed took a close look at his brother's condition. He'd already seen the sickness in Tommy's face. Now he looked at what was left of the leg. The stump was a charred, blackened lump of a thing, oozing pus and watery blood from crevasse-like cracks in the burnt flesh. But worse still was the flesh above the cauterized area; it was bloated and sickly green, puffed up so much that the skin was stretched tight, looking fit to burst. Fluid roiled and swam just under the surface, white and soapy. The amputation had been too little, too late; the poison they had hoped to curtail was seething through what was left of the leg, and probably through Tommy's whole system.

"You see?" Tommy said softly.

Ed saw only too clearly, and now he too had tears in his eyes.

"I'm still not leaving you," he said. He called for Danny. "Please, have a look at this. Can anything be done?"

It took the soldier all of five seconds, and Ed saw the look in his face and knew the answer before he spoke.

"It's only a matter of time," Danny said, his tone grim. "It's in his blood, what's left of it."

Danny turned to the older brother.

"We haven't seen eye to eye, lad," he said. "But for what it's worth, I'm sorry it's come to this. It's no way for a man to die."

Danny turned away again, and Ed knew he was being given time with his brother, perhaps the last time they would have together. He had no idea what he was going to say until it all came out in a gush.

"This is all my fault. Me and that stupid map. I wish I'd never found it. I want no part of it now."

He took off the ring and put it on Tommy's finger.

Tommy smiled thinly, then coughed, bringing up bubbling sputum.

"Leave me, Ed. You shouldn't see me like this."

"I'm not going anywhere," Ed said.

He took Tommy's hand, like grasping a bit of hot meat. Tommy smiled again then, between one breath and the next was gone, his head rolling back and his hand going limp.

"Tommy!" Ed shouted, and grabbed his brother by the shoulders. It was like shaking a doll.

Tommy had gone on a new journey of his own.

The others stood to one side and left him alone with the body. It was several minutes before Ed could get his weeping under control and several more before he turned to address Danny.

"We're not leaving him for any beast's breakfast," he said. "We're just not."

"There are enough stones for a cairn," Stefan said.

"No," Ed replied vehemently, remembering the strewn bones where they had found the remains of the knight. "No cairn." He turned to Danny. "Can we burn him? I know it's not a Christian burial, but it's clean."

Danny nodded.

"That might be for the best. I'll take care of it, if you'd rather?"

"No, it's my responsibility, my duty."

Ed bent and kissed Tommy's forehead. It had already gone cold, the heat had gone with his spark.

Stefan passed him the flint and some tinder than the shepherd and the soldier went outside. Elsa stayed with Ed, as if realising he needed the company, while he attempted to get a small fire going against one wall of the inner canopy. It took several attempts but finally there was a tiny flame, then a larger one as it took hold. Ed had to step back as a sheet of fire washed up the inner wall. He had one last look at Tommy. The last thing he saw before the heat forced him out was the gold ring on Tommy's finger, turning red where it reflected the fire.

By the time Ed reversed out of the gorse with Elsa following him, the copse was well ablaze.

He stepped back to be beside the other two men and they watched in silence as Tommy's funeral pyre sent a cloud of smoke across the cavern.

"Ashes to ashes," Ed said, and those were the only words he spoke while the fire raged and the last of Tommy went up with the smoke and was scattered across the cavern.

They waited until the fire burned itself out. By that time, the smoke had reached up to where the great bats were roosting, causing them to fall from the roof and spiral in a flock down towards the embers.

"Time to go, lad," Danny said.

When the other two began to walk away, Ed joined them with Elsa at his side.

He didn't look back.

When Ed finally spoke, it was to relay a decision he'd made some minutes before.

"I'd like to wear his guns, if I may?" he said.

Stefan was only too happy to oblige.

"They were getting too heavy for these old bones to carry in any case."

They stopped at a meandering curve in the stream while Ed strapped on the belt and holsters. Behind them, a thin plume of smoke still rose from Tommy's funeral pyre and the bats still circled lazily overhead, but after one last look, Ed turned his back on it. He checked that the pistols were snug against his hips, tightening the belt to take up slack, then turned to Danny.

"If that beast comes back, I want to have the first shot at it," he said.

The old soldier looked as if he might argue, but he must have seen the determination in Ed's face, for he merely nodded.

"If we're given the chance, of course. The kill will be yours."

Ed didn't just want to kill the thing that had taken his brother; he wanted to blow its brains out and dance amid the ruin of its skull. A red rage boiled in him that he'd never felt before, but it was something he could use to keep him moving, to keep his grief at bay until he had time to give it room in his head. For now, the fire of anger blotted out all else.

Again, Danny must have seen something in his face. He put a hand on Ed's shoulder.

"Let's get the hell out of here, what do you say, lad? I've had enough of scrambling around in the gloom with God knows how many tons of rock hanging over my head. I need some sun, a few beers, and a decent meal that isn't something that looks like a rabbit. Let's go find it."

They turned back to their trail, walking into the breeze that was ever-stiffening in their faces.

- 15 -

Danny knew that his attempt to gee up the lad had been more for Ed's sake than his own; since the death of the older brother, Danny was getting more and more convinced that they were indeed on the wrong path and that descending any farther was madness. But he could see no other recourse; there was no way out the way they had come, and following the breeze had to be their best bet.

It was just that he couldn't get his gut to believe it.

At least Ed hadn't collapsed into a shell of grief; the lad had taken the lead and was setting a brisk pace along the side of the stream. Stefan and Elsa followed next; the dog, as if aware of the sombre mood that had fallen on the travelling companions, stayed at the shepherd's heel and even the occasional rustle in the grass wasn't enough to make her leave the man's side.

Danny brought up the rear, chewing on the tattered remains

of a cheroot. He didn't know how long they'd been in this godforsaken hole, but he knew it had been long enough that he was nearly out of smokes and that he was bone tired, his body telling him he should be asleep. He guessed it was nighttime again, somewhere far above, and that if they were lucky enough to get out soon, it would be the moon rather than the sun they'd be seeing. At the moment, he'd welcome either.

After twenty minutes walking, it became clear that they were finally approaching the far end of this current cavern. The roof began to close down above them, the bats no longer circled overhead, having returned one by one to their roosting spots, and the stream was flowing faster now, picking up speed as the downward incline got steeper.

The breeze was a full-on wind now, tugging at Danny's clothes and sweeping his hair up at his forehead. It smelled fresh with no hint of corruption in it and for the first time in a while, he felt the stirrings of hope. It appeared that the others had similar feelings for young Ed picked up the pace even further at the front, Stefan and Elsa followed suit and all of them were almost running when they realized that the wind was blowing out of a dark entranceway only a hundred yards ahead.

But they were forced to a halt at the cave mouth; the stream tumbled out of the cavern in an almost vertical fall at their feet, thundering away and down into darkness. Inside this new cavern, there was no sign of light, none of the dangling luminescent roots to show a possible path...there was only the roar of water and blackness in front of them.

Danny checked to either side, but the flow of water from the stream filled the whole breadth of the entrance; there would be no descent possible. Even as he came to that decision, he saw young Ed get down on his hands and knees in the water and start to inch himself backwards towards the lip.

"No, lad," he shouted, and manhandled the youth back out of the water. "Getting yourself killed fast isn't the way to get out of here."

Ed shook him away, and Danny saw the need in his gaze.

"What then? You said it yourself, the breeze is our best chance of escape. It comes from there." He pointed at the fall of water. "So there is where we must go."

"You're a climber, lad, so maybe you could do it. But I'm an old soldier, Stefan here is a shepherd... and Elsa certainly can't get down yon hole."

"We have the rope..." Ed said.

"Aye, and look where we've ended up after the last time we tied you to it. And what if there is a bottom we can reach? With no lights, what do we do then? No, we find another way."

"There is no other way!" Ed shouted.

"You're forgetting your wee map again, lad," Danny answered. "Your knights, at least one of them, got out. There is a way."

Elsa seemed to agree with Danny. She began to bark then she walked several yards to the left of the cave mouth, following the cavern wall away from the stream, then turned to look at Stefan as if to say, 'Are you stupid? Of course we go this way.'

Stefan laughed.

"She has found the scent of home again. Do not despair, young Edward. She will see us out of here, you mark my words."

The dog led the way as they headed left.

It did not take too long...no more than a minute...for Danny to see that the dog did indeed have a goal in mind. An animal trail, the horse-things judging by the droppings they had to dodge around, led to a second cave mouth. This one had no fall, no stream to block their passage. But it was as dark as the previous cave; if they were to proceed that way, it would be in darkness.

Danny remembered how they'd used clumps of the hanging roots earlier and looked around them, hoping to find a spot where they could reach up and pull some down from the roof. But although the roof was indeed lower here, it was still well out of reach for them, even if he were to stand on Stefan's shoulders. He led out a snort of disgusted frustration.

"Could we shoot some down?" Ed asked. "All fire at once and concentrate on a small area, try to dislodge a chunk?"

Danny was loath to use up ammo they might need later, but saw some sense in the lad's idea, enough to at least give it a try. He had Danny pass one of the Colts to Stefan, then pointed out a brighter patch of the ceiling some five yards above them.

"On a count of three," he said. "Three shots each. If that doesn't do it, we won't waste any more ammo and take our chances in the dark."

He took out his own pistol and took aim, counting down. They all fired on three, not quite in unison, a nine-shot volley that roared like cannon fire in the confines of the cavern. Shards of rock flew and Danny was forced to duck away. When he looked up again, it was to see a large clump of vegetation detach itself from the ceiling and fall, almost on top of them, causing all three to dance aside.

"Well bugger me sidewards," Danny said. "I would have bet my pension that wouldn't have worked. Quickly now, gather it up. We need to get moving while it's still luminescent. Get as much as you can carry."

They all sheathed their weapons again and gathered the vegetation into their arms; Stefan even managed to weave some through Elsa's collar. When they entered the cave, they saw the faint light show in the dark where she walked ahead of them.

Danny was almost congratulating himself when a roar echoed from the cavern at their back; their shots had once again alerted the wyrm to their presence…and given away their location.

"Quick as we can, lads," Danny said. "Yon beast is not giving up. And we don't know if those bats will keep it at bay a second time."

They descended a slight slope. Soon, the cave mouth was only a small circle of light at their back and they were going down into near darkness.

The going was easy at first, the ground underfoot having been smoothed by some long-since dried stream, and the vegetation in their arms proving enough dim light for them to see by, but it was already obvious that the glimmer from the roots was fading fast. Danny tried to peer ahead, searching for any glimpse of light ahead, but there was only the bobbing gleam from Elsa's collar, and that too was getting dim.

In less than another minute, Danny saw that the vegetation was now useless; he could not see the other men in front of him. He called for a halt and heard the scrape of the others' heels on rock as all three of them came to a stop. He felt something tickle at his knee and realised it was Elsa having come to heel but looking down, he saw nothing but blackness. He turned and looked back the way thcy had come. The tunnel mouth was only a pinprick, a star flickering in the distance.

"What now?" Ed whispered in the dark.

"Drop the roots," Danny said. "They're no use now."

There were several soft thuds as the vegetation hit the ground.

Danny spoke first to head off any more questions.

"Sidle over, I'll take the lead," he said. "Stay within touching range behind me, we move in step, as one, and we move slowly. We follow the left-hand wall by touch, and if I stay stop, you stop, no questions. Understood?"

He got murmurs of assent from the others, and Elsa moved against his knee, as if she too was agreeing. Danny moved past the other two men; it was a tight squeeze but when he got to the front, he was pleasantly surprised to feel a slight breeze in his face. That at least would ensure he kept some sense of direction in the dark. He considered using up his matches, but decided against it; they would only provide dim illumination at best, and they might be needed for making a fire if they ever got out of this bally tunnel.

He put his left hand on the tunnel wall and took his first step down into the dark.

- 16 -

Ed was in the middle, sandwiched between Danny in front and the shepherd behind. Elsa walked at Danny's heel and every so often, Ed would feel his right leg brush against her flank. The only sound was the soft pad of their feet on rock and Stefan's rather heavy breathing at Ed's back

Ed had never known such blackness. Even as a boy in bed, on a dark night with no candles in their room, there had always been faint glimpses of moon peeking through clouds, or the lights of the town in the valley. But here, he couldn't even see the back of Danny's head even though he knew it was two feet away at the most. Only the feel of rock underfoot and the scrape of the fingers of his left hand on cold stone assured him that he wasn't in fact floating in the vastness of the spaces between the stars.

They continued to descend for several minutes with no alarms when the howl of the wyrm rose up at their back again, louder than the last time.

"It's following. It's in here with us," Ed whispered, his right hand reaching instinctively for the butt of the Colt at his side.

"I know, lad," Danny said in front. "And if you have any good ideas, I'm all ears. If not, we go on. There is little else for it."

They continued down. The slope increased, not enough to cause them a problem, but enough to be noticeable and cause them to move even more carefully. Danny brought them to a halt five minutes later.

"I've come to an opening. Stay where you are, I'll investigate."

The next few minutes felt like an hour. At every breath, Ed imagined the wyrm barreling down the tunnel after them, imagined it coming upon them in the dark, rending and tearing before they could get a shot off. He almost screamed when a hand brushed his cheek.

"Sorry," Danny said out of the dark. "I lost my bearings there. I've found a cave, and I think it's defendable. It will give us somewhere we can bed down and get some rest; I know I need it."

"We should keep moving," Ed protested, but Stefan interrupted at his back.

"I can't go much farther, young sir. My old bones need to be still for a time."

Ed allowed Danny to have the lead again. They moved two paces downward then veered left. It immediately felt stuffy now that there was no breeze, but there was no smell of the place having been a beast's lair, just the taste of old dirt in Ed's mouth.

"Stay against the wall," Danny said. "I have a surprise."

They heard ripping and tearing noises and the tumble of sticks against stone. A minute later, there was a flare of red and orange as Danny struck a match then a further flare as fire took hold amid a pile of dried roots. The new light showed that Danny had stripped them from the ceiling of the cave a foot or so overhead where they hung, long dead and shriveled, but perfect for firewood.

"We'll keep a watch, a few hours each," Danny said. "We should all get some sleep and push on once we're rested."

Ed had hardly heard him. The firelight had shown him something else, something reflecting golden at the rear of the cave and Ed's heart was in his mouth as he stepped over towards it.

"What have you got there, lad?" Danny said.

"Another indication that my map was right all along," Ed said. "For all the good that does us now."

He waited until Danny came to join him and stepped aside to let the soldier see.

A shield emblazoned with a heraldic dragon had been wedged into a corner. Behind it, they found two stout wooden firebrands, the tops of which were black…cloth dipped in tar that had gone hard over the centuries. Below them lay a red woolen cloak, but when Danny went to lift it, it fell apart in his hands.

The soldier held up the firebrands.

"This is good news," he said.

"Aye," Ed replied. "They will light our passage, for sure."

"Nay, lad, again you don't understand," Danny replied. "They left them here, thinking they might need them on their return. But they never came back for them, and yet still they got out. There is a way out, and we're going in the right direction."

Danny insisted on taking the first watch.

"You're still walking wounded, and the shepherd is older even than I. Besides, I've done this more times than you've had hot dinners. I will be fine for a few more hours. I will wake you when I feel I can't keep my eyes open any longer."

By the time Ed lay down, with the fire between him and the entrance Stefan was already snoring, with Elsa spooned up at this side like a pair of lovers. At first, Ed thought sleep would evade him completely; every time he closed his eyes, he saw Tommy's last minutes and when he opened them, tears almost blinded him such that all he could see was a shimmering red where the fire sat and a smaller patch of red where Danny sat smoking, the tip of his cigarette showing bright in the darkness.

But eventually, tiredness overcame grief. He was called into a blessed blanket of darkness and he went to it willingly.

He woke disoriented. Someone was tugging at his shoulder.

"Tommy?" he said, a whisper of hope. Then memory crashed in around him and he looked up to see the old soldier standing over him.

"Can you take a turn, lad? I'm bushed."

Ed's chest wounds complained bitterly when he sat up too fast but the pain felt duller than it had before, and when he stood, he realised he was moving much more easily.

Unlike Tommy, who won't be moving ever again.

He pushed the thought away; grief would have to wait. He needed his wits about him if he was to stand guard…he owed it to the old soldier. He owed it to Tommy.

Danny had left a skin with some water in it and the remnants of the last of the cooked rabbit lying by the fire.

"Breakfast, and a poor one at that," Ed said, but the water tasted sweet and the rabbit was strong and gamey and went down just fine. He took up a seat with his back to the fire facing the entrance, found a battered cigarette in his shirt pocket, and lit up thankfully, taking smoke deep down into him as if it would dispel the dark thoughts swirling there.

Soon, there were two sets of snores echoing in the cave with Danny's tenor complementing the shepherd's rumbling bass. At another time, it might have amused Ed but now his thoughts were back with the pale wyrm and wondering whether it was even now creeping stealthily down the gully just outside. The fire behind him cast Ed's shadow dancing on the far wall of that gully but that was all that he could see; there was only darkness to either side. By the time he'd finished his cigarette, the thought that the beast might be right there, just out of view, was too much for him to bear.

Taking care not to make any sudden noise that might wake the others, he fetched one of the ancient firebrands and held it in the fire until the flames took. He drew the right-hand side pistol and with the brand in his other hand stepped out of the entrance into the gully.

As soon as he was fully out of the cave, he heard a movement up the slope to his right. He turned, raising his pistol, and saw his brand reflected in two great eyes that seemed to peer into his soul. Even as he took aim, the beast retreated, the slither of its flesh against stone clearly audible. The red eyes disappeared from view. Ed's right hand…his whole arm…shook with nervous tension, the barrel of the pistol waving alarming. He let the hand drop to his side but didn't holster the weapon, standing still, waiting for his heart to settle and his breath to catch.

He was already regretting not taking a shot. The thing that had ultimately killed his brother had been right there, but no amount of promises, no hardening of resolve, had prepared him for the abject terror that had gripped him at the sight of those great eyes peering into his soul.

And yet, it too was afraid. I was not the one to retreat from the confrontation.

That thought gave him strength, and a measure of hope that next time, if it came, he would be able to take the chance. What he wasn't expecting was that the chance would come immediately. A fresh rasping of flesh on stone alerted him to the fact that the beast was on the move again. He had enough time to turn side on and raise the pistol then it was right there, eyes blazing in fury.

This time, he took his shot, but didn't get a chance to see if he'd hit anything; the beast's momentum was such that it came on in a rush and he was forced to retreat. He took two steps back, hoping to step into the cave mouth but somehow he'd missed his step in the gully and went farther backward than he'd intended. His left foot didn't land on stone, only meeting empty air. He tumbled backward, off balance. He lost his grip on the firebrand, which fell for a second with him then was extinguished as the beast barreled over it.

Then he was tumbling ever faster down an increasing slope.

The beast came on in the dark after him, its howls rushing down into the blackness with them.

- 17 -

Danny came awake with a start, unsure at first whether the echo of gunfire and answering howling was a dream or reality. He knew he had not been asleep for long; he felt the tiredness drag at his bones as he sat up reaching for his pistol.

Stefan was also getting to his feet. Elsa had moved to the cave mouth and stood there, barking excitedly in counterpoint to the howling that was already fading into the distance.

"Ed?" Danny shouted, and got no reply. "Damn and blast the lad. What's he gone and done now?"

He looked for the firebrands, saw that there was only one remaining, and his heart sank.

"Edward?" Stefan asked.

"He's outside somewhere. And so is yon beast. Come on…we'd best fetch him back."

Danny had Stefan gather up their packs before leaving.

"If he's made a run for it to flee the beast, we might not be coming back this way."

He took what he could from Ed's pack and shared it between himself and Stefan. The extra load dragged at already tired shoulders as he put the pack on. He lit the firebrand from the fire, drew his pistol in his right hand, and stepped out into the gully with Elsa at his heel and Stefan at his back.

The howls of the beast came up the gully from their left, from some distance below them. They found the doused firebrand, still glowing red, several paces down the slope. Stefan bent and took it for himself.

"Don't light it yet," Danny said. "We might need to conserve them."

Together, they followed the howls downward.

The slope got steep almost immediately and became more of a scramble than a walk. Several steps farther on, they found one of the Colts. Danny passed Stefan the brand, picked up the pistol, and checked it.

"Just the one shot fired. Let's hope he's held on to the other pistol."

He holstered the Colt at his hip, took the firebrand back, and continued downward.

The beast still howled somewhere below but it sounded distant now, although whether that was because it was far off or whether there was too much rock between them there was no way for Danny to know. He could only hope that the howling was a good sign; it meant that the beast wasn't feeding...it meant there was still a possibility of them finding the lad alive.

That hope diminished slightly when Elsa brought them to a halt, sniffing around excitedly at a rock. It appeared to gleam dark in the firelight and when Danny bent for a closer look, he saw it was blood, although whether from man or beast he was unable to tell.

"Find Ed, Elsa," Stefan said. "Fetch him back to us."

The dog didn't need asking twice; she bounded away out of sight into the darkness.

"If he is in trouble, she will be of some help to him," the shepherd said in reply to Danny's glance. Danny also saw worry there but didn't speak of it for the same feeling was crawling through him from toes to crown and his gut seethed and roiled, indicating trouble ahead.

They continued down.

Silence fell below them. The flickering firebrand showed only dancing shadows ahead. They passed several cave entrances, but a quick look into each was enough to show that Ed hadn't managed to take shelter in any of them. The slope eventually evened out and became less severe, but there was still no sign of their companion, nor of Elsa. They found another patch of blood on a flatter area of ground.

"He's injured," Stefan said.

"Either him or the beast. Let's hope it's the latter."

When the attack came, it was from out of a deep-cut rift on their left that Danny had been about to explore. His instincts kicked in; almost before he was aware of seeing the red eyes, his pistol hand had come up and aimed such that when the beast's head lunged out of the dark and its mouth opened it was a perfect target. Danny put two shots down its throat, but that barely slowed it. It came forward so fast that Danny had to retreat or be buried by its weight. He thrust the firebrand into the left eye, feeling it pop under the pressure, tasting burning flesh in his throat. The beast howled in rage and pain. It tried to back away, but in its rage had got itself stuck in the cleft.

It spat blood in Danny's face and howled again, dislodging ancient dried roots from the roof in its frenzy to escape. Danny raised his pistol again, took careful aim, and put two more rounds into the remaining eye. Finally, the beast realised it was dead and went still. Danny put another bullet into its head to make sure.

His shots echoed long and loud around them then silence fell again.

Several seconds later, Elsa barked, somewhere in the dark below them.

- 18 -

Ed didn't know for how long or how far he'd fallen in the dark. He'd landed, hard, on bare rock, the landing knocking all breath out of him. All he could do was lie there and wait for the beast that he heard howling somewhere high above.

It felt as if he'd gone blind. His senses seemed to have pulled in on themselves, hiding as deep in darkness as he was himself. There was only pitch blackness in front of his eyes and the pain in his bruised body. He knew nothing else for several minutes and it was some time after that he realized that silence had fallen.

Somehow, that just made things worse.

He reached for his pistol on the right side, found an empty holster, and remembered he'd been holding the weapon when he'd fallen. He didn't have it now and wasn't about to go crawling around in the dark looking for it. The one in the left holster was still there, and he took it out, transferring it to his right hand. With his left hand, he felt his body for injury. Nothing seemed to be broken; when he sat up there was pain in his back but no grinding of bone against bone, and his legs worked when he forced himself to his feet. The movement had caused some noise which echoed faintly around him. He guessed he was still in the same gully as before, possibly at the foot of it, but without light, there was no way to know.

The wounds at his chest had opened again and the front of his shirt felt wet but feeling around inside the material he found stickiness but little fresh flow. It seemed he was alive, and likely to stay that way.

But for how long?

He considered calling out then thought better of it. He couldn't hear the beast, but he knew it had to be there somewhere and drawing attention to himself in the dark would be a quick way to suicide.

"Gillam will come for me," he whispered to himself.

It felt like a prayer of hope.

He was considering taking a step in the dark to feel for a wall when he heard a scrambling somewhere high to his right. He got as far as raising the weapon to take aim, but he was too slow, and almost leapt out of his skin when Elsa leapt up, planted her legs on his tender chest, and licked him full in the face.

"Good girl," he whispered, almost weeping at the sense of comradeship he found in the simple presence of the dog. "Where are the others?"

In reply, Elsa dropped to her paws and tugged his left-hand cuff, as if telling him to follow. He crouched, kept a hand at the scruff of her neck and together, painfully slowly, they began to climb through the dark.

They had moved only half a dozen steps when the sound of gunfire echoed through the cave system. When the echoes died down, Elsa let out two loud barks.

After several seconds, a voice called out faintly from above. It was the old soldier.

"Ed? Are you there?"

This time, there were indeed tears as he shouted out an affirmative.

"Stay where you are, we're coming to you," Danny answered. Ed fell to his knees, holding the dog tight to him, letting its warmth and simple comforts fill the dark spaces he felt inside.

Less than a minute later, he saw red-flickering shadows dance on the roof, and a minute after that saw the flame of a firebrand appear high above in the gully, with two dark figures walking there. Elsa barked excitedly, and Ed allowed the tears to come and flow freely, so much so that he had to wipe them clear to greet his companions when they arrived at the foot of the slope.

"Hail fellows, well met," he said, hearing the hitch in his voice as he spoke.

Danny grunted in reply, then smiled.

"Damn, lad, it's good to find you alive. But don't be going doing anything daft like that again."

"The beast?"

"Dead as anything I've ever shot," Danny replied. "But don't go celebrating too much; I'm guessing there's more of the buggers around here somewhere."

Ed took the firebrand while Danny reloaded his pistol and swapped it in the holster for the Colt, which he handed back to Danny.

"You dropped this," he said, and repeated his earlier words. "Don't be doing anything daft like that again."

"So what now? Back to the cave so you can get some rest?"

"Nay, lad. Yon beast might be dead, but I've no need to see it again. And can't you feel it? The breeze is stronger again here. We're getting close."

Ed had to turn his head to feel it, but the breeze was indeed stronger here, coming up through where the gulley widened at his back.

Danny clapped him on the shoulder.

"Full speed ahead, lad. Supper's waiting."

Ed allowed Stefan to check his wounds. The shepherd sucked his teeth, muttered under his breath, washed away dried blood with some water and a handkerchief, then declared Ed to be fit enough to move on.

"If we have to run, he will bleed again, and bad at that."

Danny grimaced.

"Let's make sure we don't have to run then." He held up the firebrand. The breeze was enough to set the flames flickering wildly. "Are you ready to move, lad?"

That last was addressed to Ed. He felt stiff and sore, but his legs worked just fine. When Danny headed into the breeze, Ed followed right behind him.

He realised as they walked that he was listening for sounds of pursuit, still fearing attack from the wyrm.

"Are you sure it's dead?" he said.

"As sure as I am of anything," Danny replied. "I know you wanted the honor, but I didn't have time for niceties. If it helps to know, I took it down with your brother's gun, so if you are looking for a measure of revenge, find it in that."

Ed fingered the butt of the pistol at his hip.

"We got it, Tommy," he whispered, but if Tommy was somewhere listening, he didn't reply.

They descended into the dark.

Ed was calculating their descent in his head, and he didn't like the results he was getting, but the outcome came out the same every way he looked at it.

"We've come down too far," he said. "Much farther than we climbed from the village. We are below ground level by now, surely?"

Danny took his time in replying and when he did, he was grave.

"Aye, I know. And my gut tells me we're going in the wrong direction too. But we've made the correct decision at every opportunity on the way. I cannot see any other course but to follow our noses. Mayhap we will come out further down one of the mountain valleys. Yon stream has to come out somewhere."

Ed knew that streams in caves didn't necessarily emerge in the open but he held his peace; like the old soldier, he could see no other course of action but to follow the breeze and hope. Hope was about all Ed had left.

The breeze continued to strengthen. There was a definite smell to it now. Ed tasted brine at his lips.

"Salt water? But we are many leagues from any sea."

"Let's not second guess ourselves," Danny said, but Ed saw the same concern in the man's face that he felt in himself.

Several minutes later, they began to see dim light far ahead of them, and it brightened quickly as they approached what appeared to be an opening out of the cave.

Danny let out a yelp of joy.

"I told you, lad. Didn't I tell you?"

They were almost running as they approached the light and Ed came close to knocking Danny over when the old soldier came to a sudden halt in the cave mouth. Ed saw why when he looked over Danny's shoulder to the scene beyond.

Far from having escaped the cave system, it appeared they had emerged into an even larger, more complex part of it. A ceiling of rock festooned with luminescent roots hung a hundred yards overhead, arching over an underground lake that stretched away into an unimaginable distance with no apparent far edge that Ed could discern. A flock of the giant bat-things wheeled lazily just below the ceiling, the only things moving in the landscape save for a gentle ripple on the shimmering surface of the water.

Elsa barked at Ed's side, and he looked down to see that she was looking over to the right. A high path led away from where they stood around this side of the lake and upwards slightly to a ledge overlooking the lake from a higher vantage. Then he saw what had caught the dog's attention; they were not the first people to see this scene. Someone had been here before them in some distant past, and had left a marker of their presence, a tall roughly hewn stone cross atop a large mound of piled stones.

Ed saw that Danny was looking the other way. To the left, a path wound down the cliff towards a shoreline fifty yards below. A rough forest of pale distended woodland filled an area between the cavern floor and the water. There was no sign of life there either.

Ed brought the old soldier's attention to the right-hand path. Without another word, Danny extinguished the firebrand and set off at a brisk walk around the path towards the cross.

- 19 -

On his first sight of this new cavern, Danny's hopes of a quick escape had been dashed so completely that he considered, for longer than he would admit to himself, just stepping forward, two small steps was all it would take, then a quick fall into oblivion.

He couldn't do it, not just because he felt an obligation to his companions, but because the old soldier in him wasn't used to admitting defeat without a fight and there was nothing to strike against here but himself. When Ed pointed out the stone structure on the ledge, he saw it as a sign of renewed hope. They were still on the right track; they just hadn't quite reached the end of it yet.

By the time they were getting close to the stone cross, the track had widened enough that they could travel two abreast, and Danny wasn't in the least bit surprised when Ed went past him, almost at a full run, with an excited Elsa at his heel. When Danny caught up with him, he was at the cross, moving rocks aside. He turned, and Danny saw disappointment in his face.

"It's not there. There's no treasure. It's just stones."

"Aye. A marker to show anyone who followed they were heading in the right general direction, I expect. Better than carving marks on the walls at any rate."

Elsa had kept moving when Ed stopped. She now stood in front of the cave beyond the cross, her hackles raised, growling softly at the back of her throat. Stefan went to try to calm her.

"She's shaking like a leaf," the shepherd said as he stroked her flank. "I think there's something in there."

Danny handed Ed the extinguished firebrand, had him hold it while he lit it from a match, then drew both his pistol and his sword.

"I think there's something in there too," he said. "But unless we fancy a long swim, it's the way we have to go. Ed, stay close behind me with that flame. And watch my moves. I don't want anything to get in my way if I have to shoot."

The firebrand lit the passage ahead of him in flickering shadow but it quickly became clear it wasn't going to be required. Little more than ten yards into the side of the cliff, it opened up into a new chamber. Ed gasped at Danny's back.

"Danny?"

"I see it, lad. No sudden moves. Not if you want to live."

They were looking into a vast, cathedral-like cavern

festooned with more of the dangling, luminescent roots. The walls were smooth and showed signs of axe and hammer markings; if it had been a natural chamber at one time, it had also been enhanced. That wasn't the main thing that caught the eye though.

They had found Ed's long-sought treasure, a mound of gold, silver, and jewels piled in the center of the room, as large as the mound outside on which the cross had been mounted.

But again, that wasn't what had caused their consternation. The chamber was dominated by a huge pale wyrm that lay coiled atop the treasure mound. Its barrel-like body looked to be six feet or more in diameter, its vast head almost as broad and wide as the entrance in which they stood and its body, by Danny's rough estimate, at least forty feet from nose to tip of tail.

It appeared to be asleep.

Ed nudged Danny and pointed, past the sleeping beast to the far wall of the chamber. Looking incongruous and far out of its natural place, a roughly hewn wooden door was fitted flush to the stone.

Danny motioned that the others should fall back and several seconds later, they had returned to stand below the tall cross outside.

"A bloody dragon on a mound of treasure," Danny said. "Have we fallen into a fairy tale?"

"Or perhaps we have found the original source of the

legend?" Ed replied. "But either way, the question remains the same—what do we do now?"

"We let sleeping beasties lie, that's what we do now. But I'm going to have to find out what's on the other side of that door. It may be our hope of escape to the surface."

"And it may be a lavatory," Ed said. "The risk is great."

"But the reward, if it means our freedom, will be worth it."

Danny double-checked that his pistol was fully loaded then addressed the others.

"You should stay in the entranceway. Ed, give Stefan one of the pistols; we may need all the firepower we can muster if yon beastie wakes before I reach the door. Either way, if it comes to it, don't try any heroics; save yourselves if I get into trouble."

He didn't wait; he knew they'd only try to talk him out of his course of action, just as he knew it wouldn't take too much talking to get him to retreat all the way down to the sea and see how that went. His legs felt weak at the knees as he walked along the passageway and emerged again to face the sleeping beast.

It smelled, a musty, slightly vinegary odor that stung at the back of his throat. The massive torso swelled and contracted with each inhale and exhale of breath. The merest glimmer of a red eye showed under the left eyelid, and the tail—too small a word for a lump of muscle and bone that would crush a man in an instant—swung lazily against the gold and jewels causing them to clink and rattle with a rhythm that was almost musical.

Danny stood in the entrance for at least a minute attempting to convince himself that the beast was indeed asleep and not just pretending in an attempt to lure him into the chamber. Elsa brushed against his right knee; it appeared she had decided he needed protection. He welcomed the company and it stiffened his resolve to take the first step, moving to his left to hug the wall at the side of the entrance.

The wyrm swung its tail again but there was no other sign of movement. Feeling buoyed up with that, Danny shuffled around the perimeter of the cavern, keeping his back to the wall and his pistol aimed at the wyrm's left eye. Elsa kept a close companion at his side, her own gaze never leaving the beast.

The worst point was halfway round towards the door when they were nearest to the beast's head. Danny felt the heat of its breath against his cheeks, like standing in front of an open oven door, with the smell of meat wafting at the same time. The left eye twitched, so much so that Danny's finger moved to the pistol's trigger, but after a single slip and slide of the tail that sent some gold coins tinkling across the floor, the beast was still again. Danny took a breath he hadn't realised he'd been holding off. He kept moving, concentrating on placing his feet down softly and making sure nothing, his scabbard in particular, was going to hit the wall and raise a sound.

When he finally reached the old wooden door several minutes later, he allowed himself several seconds of relative relaxation.

He hadn't given any thought what he might do if the door was firmly locked against them, but that worry was misplaced.

When he put a hand on a handle and pulled the old door swung open, an alarming creak echoed around the chamber.

Danny's heart leapt to his mouth and again his finger moved to cover the pistol's trigger, but apart from another swing of the tail, the beast still showed no signs of waking. Danny turned his attention to what was on the other side of the door.

A roughly hewn set of stone steps led upwards at a steep angle. It was dark in there, but when he stepped inside and looked upward he saw a faint pinpoint of light, far up in the distance, but shining and golden in a way he hadn't seen since entering the cave system; he knew, without doubting, that he was looking up at the outside world and the means of their escape.

He went back to the doorway and motioned that the others should come across to join him.

Stefan came first. Like Danny before him, he kept his pistol aimed at the beast. Elsa watched his every move and Danny sensed the tension in the dog that was only released when the shepherd joined him in the doorway. Danny made a mummer's play of showing Stefan that he should go up the stairs a way, light the firebrand, and wait for him and Ed. He did it all without speaking, but the older man seemed to get the gist well enough and headed off into the stairwell until all Danny saw of him were his ankles. Elsa stayed at Danny's side as Ed started his circumnavigation of the chamber.

Ed was moving slower than either of the previous two men and his pistol wavered between pointing at the floor and aiming vaguely at the beast, but at least he was moving, and Danny thought they had a good chance of getting away with it.

Then Ed broke from the plan. He moved away from the wall and stepped forward. At first, Danny thought he meant to make a go at killing the beast in misplaced revenge for his brother. Then he saw the youth's real intent.

Ed was going for some of the treasure, right beneath the beast's nose.

- 20 -

There had been little conscious thought in Ed's action. He'd been concentrating on getting round to join Danny at the door without mishap but the wyrm's tail had swished again, dislodging some rubies that scattered on the floor, the red reflecting the dim light from the ceiling and making them appear like small glistening chips of dried blood.

Just one, one for a keepsake. One for Tommy.

And even as he had the thought, he had stepped forward.

He took his eye off the beast, bent, and plucked a ruby the size of his thumb off the floor. When he looked up again, he was looking directly into the open eye of the wyrm.

Like his first action, there was little thought in his next. He brought up the Colt, aimed, and fired all in one movement. It was too big a target even for him to miss. A small red hole showed above the beast's right eye, and the head jerked with the impact, but the respite was only momentary. Shaking itself like a dog waking from a nap, the beast reared up, looming yards above Ed's head.

"Run, you bloody fool," Danny shouted from the doorway, and suddenly Ed found impetus where there had been none before. He threw himself under the jaw of the beast as it was reaching for him and with legs pumping like pistons made it to the doorway just ahead of it. Danny had already retreated inside and was trying to hold Elsa off from attacking while at the same time trying to get a shot past Ed towards the beast.

"Don't wait for me," Ed shouted. "Get going, I'm right behind you."

He pushed Danny up the first few stairs, turned, and fired two shots without aiming, without needing to for the bulk of the beast filled the doorway, then was off and scrambling up a dark, almost pitch black stairwell.

The wyrm's howls roared as loud as any pistol shot, almost deafening. The stairwell narrowed, and narrowed again until Ed's shoulder's touched the walls. Twice he was kicked in the head as Danny scrambled above him. A new sound from below made him look down; it was dim, but he was just able to make out the wyrm, trying to force its head into the passageway. There came a grinding and tearing, talons on stone, as it began to dig, determinedly. The walls of the stairwell rocked and shook and pebbles, then larger-sized pieces of rock tumbled around the climbing men.

"Climb. Climb like your lives depend on it," Danny shouted, and Ed didn't need a second telling. He was about to take another step up when something grabbed, hard, at his left ankle and tugged, taking him down to elbows and knees. He turned and saw that the beast's long, flexible tongue had him around the ankle and the beast's head was only three feet away. Its breath was foul and hot, its red eyes gleamed in triumph as it tugged again and Ed was drawn backward towards waiting teeth.

He turned fully onto his back, aimed the pistol between his legs, pointing directly down the beast's throat.

"This is for Tommy, you bastard," he said, and fired three quick shots directly into the maw. The pressure on his ankle lifted away immediately as the beast recoiled and drew back. Ed didn't wait to see what happened to it. He turned back to the steps and climbed for all he was worth.

Beneath him, the beast howled, and attacked the entrance with even more vigor than before. More stones fell around them. Ed heard Stefan let out a yelp of pain and guess one had got him on the head, but all three kept climbing, although the whole stairwell rocked and rolled as if in the grip of an earthquake. The bellows of the beast followed them upward.

Ed's chest wounds opened again. He felt the blood's heat beneath his shirt. And as if the smell of it had permeated down the shaft, the beast below increased its frenzied attack. It sounded closer and Ed's imagination ran wild, imagining it slithering like a great snake, pushing itself along up the narrow passageway, its teeth even now reaching for his feet. He tried to increase his tempo, but his pace was determined by Danny above him, and Stefan above that, and the man at the top appeared to have slowed to little more than a crawl.

And still they climbed. More debris came from above, threatening to block the passage completely. And still the beast raved and howled somewhere below them. Ed's existence narrowed to forcing his way upward, in pitch blackness now, the steps uneven in height making it difficult to gauge where his feet should be placed. The dust tasted like ash in his throat. He closed his eyes against it; they were useless in the darkness anyway, and forced himself upward.

Finally, Ed could go no further. His legs were like jelly beneath him, the tumbling rock and dirt from above threatened to grab him around the waist and block him there like a cork in a bottle. He opened his mouth to call out and it immediately filled with dirt. There was one last bellow of rage from below, the whole shaft shook, and Ed felt himself begin to slide backward.

He was almost ready to give himself to the dark when he felt a strong hand grip his arm and tug. Bright light pierced his eyelids and as he was pulled roughly up and out of the hole, he felt sunlight on his face, although opening his eyes to it proved almost blinding after the gloom in the stairwell.

He stood, in the valley floor to the south of the village, looking up at the mountain they had been below.

Even then, the ground continued to heave and shake like sea in a storm. There was a rumble like distant thunder, a final, far-off howl of rage from the wyrm, then the ground all around them fell, a yard all at once, knocking them off their feet.

Then everything went still. Ed struggled to his feet to see Elsa running around in open grassland like a happy puppy and Danny and Stefan hugging each other, both with grins beaming from ear to ear.

Ed looked for signs of the stairwell, but the ground had been changed so utterly, had fallen in on itself to such a degree, that there was no trace left of their exit.

"Well, lad," Danny said. "We made it. And as I am still under your contract, my suggestion now is that we head for some ale and some decent meat before starting the long road home. What do you say?"

What Ed wanted to say was that he'd be back; the treasure was there, he'd seen it, had been close enough to touch it. And rock fall or no rock fall, he knew that there was a way to reach it by going back over the same route again. He would raise another expedition and the ruby that nestled in his shirt pocket would pay for it; that, and a decent burial for his brother when they retrieved what was left of his bones.

But that wasn't what Danny needed to hear. Ed clasped the old soldier by the arm and pointed him toward the village.

"Lay on, MacDuff. I believe it's your round."

THE END

THE LAND BELOW

CHECK OUT OTHER GREAT DINOSAUR THRILLERS

SPINOSAURUS
by Hugo Navikov

Brett Russell is a hunter of the rarest game. His targets are cryptids, animals denied by science. But they are well known by those living on the edges of civilization, where monsters attack and devour their animals and children and lay ruin to their shantytowns.

When a shadowy organization sends Brett to the Congo in search of the legendary dinosaur cryptid Kasai Rex, he will face much more than a terrifying monster from the past.

Spinosaurus is a dinosaur thriller packed with intrigue, action and giant prehistoric predators.

LAND OF DEATH
by Eric S Brown & Alex Laybourne

A group of American soldiers, fleeing an organized attack on their base camp in the Middle East, encounter a storm unlike anything they've seen before. When the storm subsides, they wake up to find themselves no longer in the desert and perhaps not even on Earth. The jungle they've been deposited in is a place ruled by prehistoric creatures long extinct. Each day is a struggle to survive as their ammo begins to run low and virtually everything they encounter, in this land they've been hurled into, is a deadly threat.

CHECK OUT OTHER GREAT
DINOSAUR THRILLERS

WRITTEN IN STONE
by David Rhodes

Charles Dawson is trapped 100 million years in the past. Trying to survive from day to day in a world of dinosaurs he devises a plan to change his fate. As he begins to write messages in the soft mud of a nearby stream, he can only hope they will be found by someone who can stop his time travel. Professor Ron Fontana and Professor Ray Taggit, scientists with opposing views, each discover the fossilized messages. While attempting to save Charles, Professor Fontana, his daughter Lauren and their friend Danny are forced to join Taggit and his group of mercenaries. Taggit does not intend to rescue Charles Dawson, but to force Dawson to travel back in time to gather samples for Taggit's fame and fortune. As the two groups jump through time they find they must work together to make it back alive as this fast-paced thriller climaxes at the very moment the age of dinosaurs is ending.

HARD TIME
by Alex Laybourne

Rookie officer Peter Malone and his heavily armed team are sent on a deadly mission to extract a dangerous criminal from a classified prison world. A Kruger Correctional facility where only the hardest, most vicious criminals are sent to fend for themselves, never to return.

But when the team come face to face with ancient beasts from a lost world, their mission is changed. The new objective: Survive.

CHECK OUT OTHER GREAT DINOSAUR THRILLERS

JURASSIC ISLAND
by Viktor Zarkov

Guided by satellite photos and modern technology a ragtag group of survivalists and scientists travel to an uncharted island in the remote South Indian Ocean. Things go to hell in a hurry once the team reaches the island and the massive megalodon that attacked their boats is only the beginning of their desperate fight for survival.

Nothing could have prepared billionaire explorer Joseph Thornton and washed up archaeologist Christopher "Colt" McKinnon for the terrifying prehistoric creatures that wait for them on JURASSIC ISLAND!

K-REX
by L.Z. Hunter

Deep within the Congo jungle, Circuitz Mining employs mercenaries as security for its Coltan mining site. Armed with assault rifles and decades of experience, nothing should go wrong. However, the dangers within the jungle stretch beyond venomous snakes and poisonous spiders. There is more to fear than guerrillas and vicious animals. Undetected, something lurks under the expansive treetop canopy . . .

Something ancient.

Something dangerous.

Kasai Rex!

Manufactured by Amazon.ca
Acheson, AB